The Body in the Bathtub

Viola Roberts Cozy Mystery Book 4

Shéa MacLeod

The Body in the Bathtub

DEDICATION

For my bunco girls:
Dreamis
Kathy
Marian
Patti
Carrie
Charline
Mariane
Diana
Joan
Marcia
Diane
Sorry I had to kill some of you… ;-)

.

Chapter 1
Matchmaking Machinations

"Darling, I sat next to the nicest man at the coffee shop the other day." My mother sat down across from me in a flurry of Chanel perfume and magenta chiffon skirts. The bright colors and light fabrics weren't exactly suitable to the chill, wet weather of a coastal Oregon winter. Her only compromise was a pair of knee-high leather boots. She stood out in the rustic setting of Caffeinate (my favorite Astoria coffee shop) like a peony among dandelions. Her hair—originally dark brown like mine—was dyed a rich burgundy and tumbled from beneath a floppy felt hat and shimmered beneath the Edison style light bulbs hanging from the tin tile ceiling.

Mom had come over from Portland to visit me for the day. She didn't like staying overnight in Astoria, preferring the three-hour round trip instead. Four-star hotels weren't good enough for her, I guess. I could have put her up in my Victorian cottage, but she steadfastly refused. She was a firm believer that overnight stays ended in blood and tears. With my mother, that was entirely possible.

Widowed at the young age of sixty, my mother— Vanessa Roberts—had taken up several hobbies which came and went like fruit flies. The entire family was relieved when she finally sold her pottery wheel at a garage sale. A person could only use so many lopsided cereal bowls. Her long-standing and most favorite hobby was playing matchmaker for her single daughter. Which would be me, Viola Roberts, romance novelist and amateur sleuth. I was still hoping she'd lose interest as she had with pottery.

I stared at her over the rim of my coffee mug, wondering how hard I should brace myself. Mornings were not my forte under any conditions. My mother was a more challenging condition than most. I decided non-committal was the best option. "Mmm-hmm."

She sighed dramatically, rolling her eyes toward the ceiling. The tiles, stamped with a fleur de lis pattern, added a touch of elegant Victorian to the rough brick walls and the wide plank floors. "Really, Viola." She flicked an invisible crumb off the table with a moue of distaste.

"What? What did I do?"

"So, anyway," she continued as if I hadn't spoken. "This man I met. He's French. Accent and everything. And…" she leaned forward, her pearls sliding dangerously close to her coffee. "He owns a winery."

"Um, okay." I wasn't sure why that was important, but from her tone she found it to be the most exciting thing ever. I inhaled the aroma of roasted magical beans before taking a fortifying sip. I was sure I was going to need it. Maybe a shot of espresso, too.

My mother ripped open a packet of fake sugar and daintily sprinkled half of it into her coffee cup, then folded the top and carefully set it aside. "I showed him your picture and gave him your number."

"Mother!" I sat back, appalled. "Why would you do that? You can't go giving out my number to random strangers. What if he's a serial killer?"

"He owns a winery." As if that somehow excused any possible sin he might commit.

I rubbed my forehead. I had a headache forming. "Mom, I'm seeing someone."

"Really?" Her eyes widened and a ridiculous grin spread across her magenta painted lips. She adjusted her hat and sat back smugly. I noticed its enormous bow matched her skirt. "Do tell."

Yep. Definitely a headache. "Remember that writer's conference I went to in Florida back in October?"

"The one where you nearly got yourself killed?"

I'd like to say she was exaggerating, but unfortunately in this case she wasn't. A double murderer pushed me down a set of marble stairs, nearly making me victim number three. "I met Lucas there," I said, deciding to ignore her comment. "We've been sort of casually seeing each other since."

"Why am I only just hearing about this now?" she demanded.

"Uh..." Because I wanted to avoid this situation. "I wasn't sure where it was going."

"Is he gay?"

"What?" I stared at her dumbly. It was way too early in the morning for this.

"Well, it's been what? Seven months now? Eight? And it's still casual? What's his problem?"

Actually, it had been over a year. "He doesn't have a problem, mother."

"Ah." She nodded in understanding. "It's you. Really, Viola. You need to get over whatever it is this is." She waved her hand in the air as if shooing a fly.

"I have no idea what you mean."

She gave me a narrow-eyed stare. "This problem you seem to have with men."

Was bashing my head against the table an option? "I don't have a problem with men."

She arched one perfectly groomed eyebrow— which reminded me I hadn't had mine waxed in a while. "Really, Viola. Need I remind you the last time you had a date was in the last decade?"

"I want to take things slow," I explained. "Not rush into anything."

"If you go any slower, you're going to turn into a glacier."

I took a sip of coffee before I said something I might regret later. "Might" being the operative word. I love my mother, but lordy, she can get on my last nerve. And she calls me the dramatic one.

"Now there's a relationship headed for disaster."

"Seriously, mother? You haven't even met Lucas."

She laughed lightly. "No. Over there." She tilted her head toward the giant plate glass windows. I could see the Columbia River as it rushed into Young's Bay before surging out to sea. Outside rain dripped from a leaden sky. Typical January day in Astoria. I tugged my navy cardigan a little closer despite it being perfectly warm inside Caffeinate.

At a table nearby, a young couple I didn't recognize was having a quiet-but-vehement argument. It was impossible to make out their words over the old school jazz coming from the speakers, but their tones were of the angry variety, their faces plastered with scowls to match. The girl looked like she'd stepped out of an '80s Goth group complete with fishnet stockings and black lipstick. The boy looked like an ordinary teenager in jeans and a plain red t-shirt. His shaggy golden hair looked like he'd just rolled out of bed.

"Who says they're in a relationship?" I asked.

"Please, darling. I know a relationship when I see one. Now tell me more about this Lucas. What's his last name?"

I mumbled something under my breath.

"Speak up. That caterwauling is ear shattering."

The music was set at a totally reasonable volume and B.B. King was not known for caterwauling. "His last name is Salvatore."

She sat forward abruptly her hazel eyes wide. "Lucas Salvatore?"

"Shhh." I glanced around but no one had noticed. Everyone in the entire city of Astoria knew Lucas and I were dating, but I didn't want to churn up the gossip mill.

"My daughter is dating Lucas Salvatore? Oh, that's almost better than a winery."

"If you say so." Lucas was a world-famous, best-selling thriller writer. Like the real life Richard Castle. Only hotter, if you can image anyone being hotter than

Nathan Fillion.

"Tell me everything." She sat back with glee. Clearly she was in for the long haul.

Bracing myself for a lengthy interrogation, I spilled my guts. Well, I left a few parts out, but I told her the most important bits about how we met and some of our dates and whatnot. Halfway through the story, the young man of the arguing couple got up and stormed out. The girl hopped up and followed him. Just another Astoria incident of no importance.

"So, when are you going to see him next? I'd love to meet him."

I bet you would. "Not sure." The idea of Lucas meeting my mother sent a chill up my spine. Granted, he would probably handle it just fine. He was used to crazed fans and pushy agents. It was me I was worried about. More than once in my life, my mother's nosiness had sent a boyfriend running for the hills. Maybe I wasn't ready to play house with Lucas, but I didn't want to lose him either.

"So, I'm working on my next book," I blurted, hoping to distract her.

She rolled her eyes. "Not more of that bodice-ripper stuff."

I write historical romances. The kind with cowboys and mail-order brides and, yes, the occasional ripped bodice. Can't write a sex scene without a rent garment or two. My mother was into crime fiction and thrillers, though I suspected she had a secret stack of romances somewhere. She was too obsessed with my relationships not to have read up on modern dating and romance.

"The usual."

"It keeps you out of trouble at least."

"And pays the bills," I said dryly. My mother had never quite gotten over the fact that I had quit my boring but highly paid accountant position to write romances. Even proof that I made more as a writer than an accountant hadn't swayed her. "Besides, I can't imagine what trouble you're talking about."

"Really, Viola. Murder?" She tsked. "It's so distasteful. And dangerous. It's a wonder you haven't been killed."

She had no idea. Recently I'd been run off the road by a killer for getting too close to the truth. Ironically thanks to that incident, I'd actually discovered the truth, and that particular killer was languishing in jail. Even more recently, someone had tried to frame me for poisoning half the town. Fortunately no one had died and the poisoner was locked up where she couldn't hurt anyone else.

"No murders. All quiet on the home front."

"You'd think in a Podunk town like this, things would be calmer."

She had a point. Not that Astoria was Podunk. It was a nice little town of about twenty thousand people located on a particularly stunning stretch of the Oregon coast. The population expanded in the summer as visitors from Portland flooded the streets in an attempt to get away from the heat of the big city. Tourists from around the globe dropped in to see the locations where Goonies and Kindergarten Cop were filmed.

"One murder doesn't constitute a hotbed of crime, you know."

"If you say so." She took a last sip of coffee. "Now, shall we hit the town? I fancy a bit of shopping. Let's visit that cute little bookstore. What's it called? Linda's?"

"Lucy's."

"That's the one." She collected her purse and umbrella and stood, waiting impatiently for me to finish my coffee.

"This seems like an interesting place," Mom said, pausing outside one of the shops along Bond Street. Bond ran between Commercial Street and Marine Drive, which ran parallel to the Columbia River. It was the heart of Astoria's downtown shopping district which ran for all of seven blocks. But it was seven blocks filled with character, coffee shops, bars, and bookstores. All the important things. And, of course, my mother had stopped in front of one of the most interesting places of all: Bartholomew's Tiki Bar.

I suppressed a groan as I followed her inside. The bar was lined with those bobbing hula dolls and edged in fake grass skirting. Multicolored lights draped from the rafters and leering Tikis loomed out from corners. There were four stools at the bar and two faux teak tables with two rattan chairs each. All of it crammed against one wall with barely enough room to walk between them. It was straight '50s kitsch, and I had to admit it was fun in a tacky sort of way.

My mother stopped in her tracks staring around her in either wonder or horror. It was hard to tell which. "How...cheerful."

The beaded curtain covering the doorway to the back room began swinging wildly and a squat woman with short, gray hair emerged. She wore a loud Hawaiian print shirt and a fake-flower lei around her neck. Her eyes lit up when she saw me.

"Viola! How are you? Haven't seen you since last month's bunco."

"Hey, Betty. How's business?"

She grinned. "Can't complain. Or I could, but who'd want to listen." She turned to my mother with a warm smile. "Welcome to the Tiki Bar."

My mother frowned. "Where's Bartholomew?"

Betty gave her a confused look. "Who?"

"The sign outside said this was Bartholomew's Tiki Bar."

Betty's expression cleared. "Ah, that. Well, Bartholomew was my father. He opened this place in 1953. He was stationed in Hawaii during The War, and when Tiki culture started booming, he decided Astoria needed to join in. We've been here ever since." She beamed proudly.

"I see." My mother's tone was a bit sharp, so I decided it was time to jump in.

"Mom, Betty is one of my bunco ladies." I played bunco—a popular dice game—once a month with eleven other women including my best friend, Cheryl. We took turns hosting, and Betty's was one of the more popular bunco destinations. Not only was her house immaculate and well decorated, but she always had the best spreads and booze. "In fact, we have a game tonight."

"Oh, how nice." Mom didn't sound like she thought it was nice.

"Why don't you jump up on one of those stools, and I'll whip you up something special," Betty suggested.

My mother perked up. "Oh, it's too early to drink."

"Pish," Betty said with a wave of her hand. "It's five o'clock somewhere. Besides, orange juice is good for you right?" She held up a carton of OJ, a broad smile on her face.

My mother brightened. "Of course. Vitamin C."

"Exactly," Betty said approvingly. She grabbed a glass and splashed in a healthy amount of juice followed by an even healthier amount of rum. Next thing I knew, Betty had brought out a big basket of crab Rangoon, and she and my mother were up to their elbows in fried wontons while my mother regaled Betty with tales of her matchmaking attempts.

Personally, it was way too early for deep-fried anything. Or rum, despite my mother's wild tales. So I stuck to hot coffee and prayed my mother wouldn't get so sloshed she couldn't drive home.

Chapter 2
Bunco Night

I finally got my mother on her way back to Portland just in time to jump in my car and head over to Agatha's house for bunco night. Fortunately, Mom had sobered up in plenty of time to drive, yet not soon enough to resume grilling me about Lucas. I still couldn't get over my mother drinking rum with Betty in a wicker chair at ten in the morning. Ammo for the next family gathering for sure.

I checked the time as I turned right on Jerome Street near the top of Coxcomb Hill and then left toward Agatha's house. A quarter to seven. Plenty of time to grab a glass of wine and some nibbles. No doubt Cheryl would already be there. Although Cheryl and I were younger than everyone else by at least two decades, bunco night was good fun and a chance to socialize with some interesting people outside our usual social circle.

Agatha lived up on the hill in one of Astoria's many Victorians. Not a little cottage like mine, but a big rambling thing complete with a wraparound porch, a turret, and powder blue siding. It nearly rivaled Flavel House in size and flamboyance. Flavel House had once been the home of Astoria's richest family, but now it was a local landmark and museum. It had also made a brief appearance in the aforementioned Goonies.

Last summer, Agatha had painted her front door bright purple and planted matching roses alongside the front walk. How she'd found so many purple roses was beyond me. Gazing balls, garden gnomes, and birdbaths were interspersed among the roses turning the garden into a hodgepodge fairyland that was truly mindboggling. With winter in full swing, the rose bushes were bare and the trees had shed their leaves. Still, the garden was no less charming.

It was still raining, so I wrapped my coat tight around me and dashed for the front porch. The door swung open before I could knock, and my best friend Cheryl stood there looking like a hotter version of Halle Berry, but with a pained grin on her face. "Thank goodness you're here." Her short, spiky brown hair was spikier than usual and she appeared a bit stressed.

"What's wrong?" I asked, tucking my purse into the hall closet after retrieving a five dollar bill for the buy-in.

"Ruby is sick tonight, so we've got a substitute."

"So?" We often had subs thanks to illness or someone being out of town. We had a few regular subs and then the odd occasional like a neighbor or relative called in at the last minute. It was really no big deal.

"It's Krys."

I frowned. "Who?"

"Krys Marlowe. Agatha's neighbor."

I tried to scrounge up some memory, but there was nothing. "I don't think I've met her before."

"You must not have because, believe me, you'd never forget her. Hazel hates her."

Hazel was one of the founding members of the bunco group and not one to go around hating people as a general rule. "Wow. What'd she do to piss off Hazel?"

"The one and only time she subbed before, she insulted Hazel's décor, dissed her dessert, and generally was loud and obnoxious."

"Wow. And Agatha invited her back?"

Cheryl shrugged. "She must have been desperate. I don't think she likes Krys. And you know what's worse?"

"Uh oh."

"Agatha forgot the wine."

We usually had a couple bottles, one red and one white, for those who imbibed. I suppose it would have come in handy in facing difficult personality like Krys.

"Come on," I said, wrapping one arm around Cheryl's shoulders. She was taller than me, so it was a little awkward. "Let's go grab something to eat. Can't be that bad."

It was. Krys was a tall woman with big hair and a bigger personality. She was loud, obnoxious, and chewed with her mouth open. "This artichoke dip isn't bad," she admitted in what my mother would call her 'outside voice.' "Would be a lot better if you added jalapeños. I went to a five-star restaurant once where they put jalapeños in the dip. Vast improvement."

I caught Edna and Hazel exchanging horrified looks. Everybody loved Agatha's artichoke dip and nobody was interested in the addition of jalapeños. I helped myself to an extra-large serving and made a show of enjoying it. Krys immediately informed me that while Triscuits were fine for artichoke dip, pita chips would be so much better. I was overly tempted to "accidentally" tip my plate of dip over her outfit.

When it was Agatha's turn to be my partner, she gave a sidelong glance at Krys over her shoulder and apologized. "I told her to behave," she said with a huff, keeping her voice low. "This is the last time. The very last time. I swear I could ring her neck. She insulted my penguins!"

Agatha had a collection of penguins displayed neatly on the mantle. The cute little birds were nested in a bed of fluffy fake snow. More winter-themed decorations crammed every inch of space in her living room: glitter-covered snowflakes hung from windows, swags of silver and gold painted holly and pinecones draped around photos of her children. It was a bit much, but a polite person would never say so. Obviously Krys was not a polite person.

I didn't share a table with Agatha until the third round. Cheryl's mom, Charlene, was my partner. Edna was Agatha's partner. Edna was overly fond of sweater sets and blinged out watches and happened to be one of the founding members of the bunco group.

I rolled the dice, got a three (which was the number for the round), and rolled again. Bunco sounds complicated, but is really pretty easy. Our game consisted of three tables of four players and we played six sets of six rounds. During each round, we rolled three dice trying to get the same number as the round. For every number rolled that matched the round number, one point was awarded to that player. If you got three of that number in one roll, that was a bunco and you won that round;

otherwise everyone kept rolling until one of the tables hit 21 points. Then that round was over and everyone switched partners to start a new round. At the end of the six sets, everyone added up their wins and buncos and the winners got prizes. Hazel used to give out actual little gifts, but everyone complained so now we just got money.

"What's Krys's deal, anyway?" I asked as I passed the dice to Edna. Agatha was an incorrigible gossip. Not a mean one; she just loved to 'share' her knowledge, and her knowledge was pretty much the shenanigans of local folk.

"Well," she said, leaning forward, excited about sharing anything remotely juicy. The strand of chunky, multi-colored beads around her neck clicked and clacked every time she moved. "She's currently married to her second husband, Malcom Marlowe. Nice man. A little vague. But I suppose you would have to be to be married to her."

I nodded in agreement. I couldn't imagine being married to someone so obnoxious. I winced as another ear-splitting cackle threatened to burst my ear drums. I guess Krys was winning.

Agatha shook her head, her short, shellacked hair not moving an inch. She'd recently had the tips frosted. How nineties. "Word has it she's estranged from her only daughter. Can't say I blame the daughter."

I couldn't either. "So besides being loud and annoying and not getting along with her offspring, anything else?"

"Oh, well, Velma hates her," Agatha said.

"You're not kidding about that," Edna chimed in. She was Hazel's best friend and privy to nearly as much gossip as Agatha, though she was less likely to share it.

I frowned. "Velma Marx? Your other neighbor?" Technically Velma lived in a Victorian two doors down from Agatha. The Marlowe house—a brick faux Tudor—was in between them. Although not a member of the bunco group, Velma had lived in the neighborhood almost as long as Agatha had. Which was longer than I'd been alive.

"That's the one. See, they both enter the Garden Beautification Contest every year," Agatha explained.

"Does that have anything to do with that ridiculous cupcake eating contest Charlie dreamed up?" Charlene, Cheryl's mom, asked. She looked a lot like Cheryl though her dark hair was slicked down instead of spiky and Charlene wore designer heels with her jeans instead of the canvas sneakers Cheryl favored.

"Probably. They're both for one of his pet charities," I said. Charlie Bayles was Astoria's mayor and was always dreaming up wild schemes to make money for various town charities like the library. Which was really great of him except they had a tendency to go wrong. Like the time he had a dance-off competition on the waterfront. It had started pouring about fifteen minutes in, but he'd insisted on continuing. That was three cases of pneumonia and a lawsuit the city didn't need. Not to mention electronic equipment not playing well with foul weather. Plus, Charlie seemed to be in it more for the glory than anything. During the summer, it was the

garden contest and the wine festival—which somehow
always got him on the front page of the paper. His latest
scheme was the Cupcake Bake-off and Eating Contest.
He'd been after me to judge it for ages. I kept dodging
him. With my luck, there'd be Ex-lax in the cupcakes or
something.

"So the Garden Contest," I prompted.

Agatha nodded. "Every year Krys wins. Gets Velma's
goat bigtime since she used to win every year until Krys
showed up in town three years ago. Velma claims Krys
has a thing going with Charlie."

"Does she?" I asked.

"Doubt it. Does he seem like her type?"

He did not, but I could sympathize with Velma. "I'm
surprised. Krys doesn't seem like a gardener." With her
long, fake fingernails and spray tan, she was definitely the
opposite of what I imagined was a gardening type.

"You didn't hear it from me," Agatha said, leaning
closer, "but she hires her garden work out. Brings in
some guy from L.A., can you believe it? He does the
design, and then she has a gardening service from
Portland do the upkeep. Can't imagine what that costs."

"Isn't that against the rules?" Charlene asked.

"Nope. Only rule is that your garden looks nice. And
Krys's garden is one of the best I've seen."

"Poor Velma," Edna tutted.

"You're telling me. Now Velma is convinced Krys will
cheat her way into winning the Bake-off. By the way,
how's the latest novel going?" Agatha gave me a pointed
look as if she knew exactly what my answer would be.

"It's...going." I'd only just started writing it a week ago.

"Well, I loved the last one. Coulda used more spice, though. I like me some spicy cowboys." Agatha winked at me.

As the sun set and the playing continued, I eventually ended up with Krys as a partner. I noticed she was suddenly quieter than she had been and she was looking a little pale. Sweat beaded her upper lip. Even her hair looked a bit wilted.

"You okay?" I asked.

"I think I must have had a bad clam at dinner." She gave me a pathetic half smile which was a big change from her earlier annoying laughter. "That's what you get for letting a man in the kitchen."

I wouldn't know. Lucas always took me out to dinner. He could cook a few basics, but then I was no stellar cook myself. I preferred baking. I mumbled something neutral and hopefully sympathetic.

"Maybe you should go home," I suggested. She really wasn't looking well and as awful as it sounded, no one would miss her.

"Oh, I'll be fine."

She didn't look fine at all. By the end of the round, she looked like she might keel over any minute. With a muttered "excuse me," she headed for the bathroom. I shrugged and continued the game with a new partner. Finally, the last round ended to a great deal of laughter. Agatha disappeared into the kitchen to get dessert ready while I helped Hazel figure out who the winners were and pass out the prize money.

"Krys came in third," Hazel said, peering at me from over the top of her red framed reading glasses. She glanced around, her tulip shaped earrings swinging wildly. "Where is she, anyway?"

"She wasn't feeling well, so she went to the bathroom. But that was like half an hour ago." I frowned, concerned for the woman. "I'll go check on her."

The bathroom was at the end of the hall, the door still shut. I knocked firmly. "Krys, you okay?" There was no answer, so I knocked louder. "Hey, Krys. Are you in there?" Still no answer. I jiggled the handle. The door wasn't locked.

Cautiously, I pushed the door open and stepped inside. At first glance the room was empty. Maybe she'd left. Gone home without telling anyone.

A horrible smell hit me, and then I saw it: One high heel shod foot sticking out of the bathtub. I stepped closer, dread pooling in my stomach. "Krys?"

Suddenly I was the one who felt sick. I moved closer and peered into the bathtub. Krys lay slumped awkwardly in the tub, unmoving, a string of vomit hanging from her mouth. I touched her wrist. No pulse. The annoying Krys Marlowe was dead.

Shéa MacLeod

Chapter 3
Enter the Bat

"I should have known you'd be in the middle of this." Detective James "Bat" Battersea loomed over me like the big, bad homicide detective he was. He was so close I caught a whiff of his woodsy cologne as he shrugged out of his heavy overcoat. I was neither amused nor intimidated. This wasn't our first rodeo. He'd been there the last time I found a body. Well, technically, I didn't find it, my friend Portia did, but I'd been there when the cops arrived.

"Hello, Batman," I said silkily.

He gritted his teeth. "You know I hate that."

I smiled. Bat's nickname came from the fact that his last name was Battersea and he'd played baseball in high school. He hated the name Bat. He hated even more that I called him Batman when the mood arose. After all, Batman—the comic book one—was referred to as the world's greatest detective. Personally, I'd go with Sherlock Holmes, but that wouldn't have been as funny.

"Are you going to be nasty? Or are you going to take my statement?" I drawled, giving him a sharp look.

He sighed and produced a notebook from the breast pocket of his dark suit. I noticed he was wearing the same yellow-and-blue tie he always wore. Seriously, the man needed a shopping trip. He might be handsome, but he had no panache when it came to dressing.

"What happened?" He might sound bored as all get

out, but his shrewd brown eyes took in everything around him.

I tapped my foot in annoyance. I knew he needed to ask questions, but time was wasting. "We were playing bunco together and Krys wasn't looking well. I asked her what was wrong, she thought she'd had a bad clam at dinner. She excused herself to go to the bathroom. When I went to check on her…" I waved my hand in the direction of the bathroom. "Well, you saw. Do you suppose she died of food poisoning? Can it kill you that fast? Or maybe she passed out and fell into the tub and hit her head." I was liking the sound of that. It explained how she ended up in Agatha's bathtub in the first place. People don't generally climb into other people's tubs in the middle of a get together, especially fully clothed.

"We'll know more after the autopsy," he said stiffly, giving away nothing. Drat him. "Is there anything else you noticed? Did she have any enemies? Did anyone threaten her?"

"I didn't actually know her. We met for the first time tonight. She was a substitute." I wasn't about to tell him about Agatha wanting to ring her neck. Or her dust up with Hazel. Neither of them would lay a finger on her except possibly in their imaginations.

Bat's eyebrows went up. "Ms. Marlowe was a sub? Who was she subbing for?"

"Ruby, one of our regulars. She's got the flu or something."

"Was this a last minute thing or…"

I shrugged. "You'd have to ask Agatha. She's the

hostess tonight so Ruby would have called her."

"I'll do that."

"Don't be getting any funny ideas about Ruby," I said. "She's a sweet woman. Wouldn't hurt a fly." In fact, Ruby was so quiet and shy, she hardly said a word on bunco nights. I couldn't imagine her having an ill thought about anyone. "Besides, this was food poisoning, right? You know what that looks like now."

"Anything else?" Bat asked, ignoring both my question and my snarky comment.

"Not that I can think of."

He flipped his notebook closed. "You can go then."

I didn't much like his dismissive attitude, but I turned to walk down the hall.

"Viola."

I turned back. "Yeah?"

"Try to stay out of this one, okay?" His expression was stern as he tried to put every ounce of command into his voice. Good luck to him.

"Long as you don't start arresting the wrong people," I snapped and stomped down the hall into the living room.

All the bunco ladies were huddled on Agatha's matching brown couches and chairs in her open plan living room. They exhibited various shades of distress while a uniformed policeman stood nearby looking lost. A couple of the women were sniffling and weepy, tissues clutched tightly in their hands. Hazel looked upset but stoic. Cheryl was comforting her mom, Charlene, one of the weepy ones. Agatha sat there playing with her beads, a stunned expression on her face.

"I can't believe someone died. In my house. In my bathtub." She shook her head, a plate of half-eaten berry pie tottering precariously in her hand. I took the pie from her and put it on the coffee table. No sense getting stains on her cream carpet.

"I'm sure Bat will figure out what happened." And I'd be helping him whether he liked it or not.

"That boy." Agatha pressed her lips together without following up with whatever it was about 'that boy' that frustrated her. It clearly spoke to her shocked state of mind. Agatha was rarely at a loss for words.

"It's going to be okay," I assured her. "I'm pretty sure Krys had food poisoning."

"People don't keel over from food poisoning, do they?" Hazel spoke up. The light glinted off the silver chain holding her reading glasses.

I shrugged. "Not like that, I don't think. But she could have gotten woozy, lost her balance, and hit her head."

"My bathtub is a killer," Agatha said with quiet drama.

"Er, maybe," I admitted. "But it's no one's fault. Just one of those crazy accidents." Not that we knew for sure it was an accident, but there was no point upsetting anyone until we had the facts.

"What's going to happen?" Rose asked timidly. She was the quietest of our group, even quieter than Ruby. A sweet woman, but not terribly outgoing. She was twisting her large ring round and round on her finger. Her husband had died a year ago and she'd recently replaced her plain wedding band with a gorgeous sapphire. Her explanation was that she'd always wanted one, but her husband had thought it frivolous and wouldn't let her have one. Once she'd mourned him properly, she'd gone out and bought herself a two-carat sapphire cocktail ring. I say three cheers for Rose.

"Bat is going to ask us all questions," I told them. "Answer honestly and everything will be fine. He's just trying to figure out what happened."

Sure enough, Bat appeared in the living room about the same time the crime scene people showed up with Mr. Voss, the local undertaker. They'd do their thing, and Mr. Voss would haul the body to the mortuary to await autopsy by the state medical examiner. Astoria was too small to have its own examiner.

"Ladies," Bat said, raising his voice a little more than necessary.

"We're not deaf, Bat," Hazel snapped, her red lips turned into a frown. "I may be old enough to be your grandmother, but I can still whip your backside." I had no doubt it was true.

He blushed, his feet shuffling slightly on the carpet. "Er, sorry." His gaze slid toward Cheryl and then quickly away before she could make eye contact.

Bat had been interested in Cheryl for quite a while. Then Duke, her high school sweetheart, showed up and they got hot and heavy, leaving Bat out in the cold. Of course that had lasted all of two minutes until Duke had freaked out and run back to Portland leaving Cheryl brokenhearted. Again. Since then, Bat had avoided Cheryl like the plague. Which I found interesting.

Bat lowered his voice to a more normal level. "I'm

going to need to speak with each of you. Ask a few questions. No big deal. Just routine. Once I've spoken to you, you may leave, but be sure to give your contact details to Officer Chambers." He nodded at the young uniform by the door. All the women turned to stare at Officer Chambers who blushed to the roots of his reddish hair. "Who wants to go first?"

Nobody moved. They all looked terrified.

Bat made a sound of exasperation. "Agatha, is there somewhere private I can have a chat with these ladies?"

"Sure, Jimmy." Jimmy? Oh my stars, really? I'd never heard anybody call Bat Jimmy. Agatha got up and led Bat to a door that opened off the living room. "My art room. It'll be quiet in here."

"Thanks, Agatha." His eagle eyes scanned the room as if trying to decide who would be his first victim.

"Rose," I said gently. "Why don't you go first?"

She looked nervous as she twisted her ring faster. "I don't know…"

"I can stay with you while you talk." I gave Bat a hard look. "Right, Detective?"

He gritted his teeth, clearly annoyed. "Actually, no. This way, Ms. Rose."

I glared at him as Rose made her shaky way across the carpet. He ignored me. Par for the course. Still, I wasn't about to give up.

"Cover for me," I whispered to Agatha as Bat shut the art room door.

"How?" Agatha's living area was what they liked to call "open concept" with the kitchen, living, and dining rooms being all in one big space. The policeman Bat had left guarding us would spot me in a flash.

"I don't know. Think of something."

She mulled it over, then jumped from the couch. "I feel sick." She marched over to the policeman looking anything but. Her mouth set in a determined line. "I need to go to my room."

"Sorry, ma'am, but Detective Battersea said…"

"I don't care what Jimmy said. I am ill. I need to lie down."

I left them arguing and crept over to the closed door. If I knelt down, I would be out of the officer's line of sight. It would also be more obvious what I was doing, but that couldn't be helped. I pressed my ear to the keyhole and listened carefully.

It was the usual thing. Did you know the victim? Did she have any enemies? And so forth and so on. Like me, Rose had just met Krys that evening and had no particular opinion other than that she was "a little on the loud side and wore too much perfume." A sentiment I most heartily agreed with. Rose was surprisingly calm for being so nervous, and the interview was quickly over. I scooted back onto the couch a split second before the door opened and Rose stepped out. The bunco ladies surged around her to offer sympathy and moral support. Everyone but Agatha who was still harassing the poor, young officer.

Next up was Betty who was as exuberant as Rose was quiet. She wore a navy and white striped sweater and white jeans with red boots. It was all very patriotic. I resumed my spot next to the keyhole.

"I didn't really know her," Betty assured Bat. "Just in passing, you know. Sometimes I'd run into her down at the grocery. On a good day she'd say 'hello' and we'd talk about the weather."

"And on a bad day?" Bat asked. I could imagine him narrowing his eyes as he latched onto something juicy.

Betty gave a light laugh, completely unperturbed by Bat's intimidation tactics. "She'd pretend she didn't know me from Adam. Just sail on by with a cart full of kale. Who actually likes kale? I mean, what do you even do with it?"

"I like kale. I have a really nice recipe for kale Caesar salad," said Agatha who had handed off the officer to Hazel and joined me at the keyhole. I held back a snicker.

"Geez," Cheryl whispered, "does Agatha have to butt into everything? She's going to end up number one on Bat's hit list if she isn't careful."

"Don't worry," I whispered back. "I think I'm already suspect number one."

"Just because you found the body?"

"Apparently I find a lot of bodies," I said dryly. It was a hard fact to argue with. I mean, technically, this was only the second body I'd found personally, but I'd managed to be in the vicinity of a number of murders. It seemed to make the police anxious.

After he finished with Betty, Bat moved through the ranks of the other bunco girls, questioning each one of them carefully. They all pretty much had the same story about barely knowing Krys. None of them particularly liked her, but they were all gracious about it, and unless Bat decided we were all in on it—whatever "it" was— the poor guy didn't have a good suspect among them.

After the women had all left except me and Cheryl, Bat questioned Agatha who repeated the Velma story about the garden contest. "Of course, Velma couldn't have killed her," Agatha said. "I mean she wasn't even here tonight, was she? Besides, she's not that sort of person."

"What sort of person?"

I was betting Agatha gave him the same look you'd give an idiot. "A killer, of course. I mean, killing over a garden? Pish. How stupid would that be? Besides, she's eighty if she's a day."

"We're not saying Ms. Marlowe was murdered, but people kill for all sorts of reasons," Bat said patiently.

"Sure they do. Why I remember the time that farmer out near Otis shot his wife in the head because she under baked a pie. Now how ridiculous is that?"

There was a pause. "That was before my time," Bat finally muttered.

"Still, you can always learn something from the past. Don't you think?"

Bat finally left, taking Officer Chambers and the crime techs with him and leaving orders not to touch the bathroom along with enough crime scene tape to ensure his orders were followed. Fortunately, Agatha had two more in her sprawling Victorian. Mr. Voss was long gone with the body and since there was no wine, Cheryl had poured us big glasses of whisky from Agatha's personal stash.

Agatha gulped hers down in two swallows and dumped more into her glass. "What a night." She leaned on the counter, propping her head on her hand. "Why did that woman have to go and die in my bathroom? I mean, how inconsiderate."

"Pretty sure she didn't mean to," Cheryl said soothingly. That was Cheryl. Always the peacemaker. Even when one of the parties was dead as a doornail.

Agatha was looking a little nervous, which I found odd. She should be relieved, having survived the interrogation. "What didn't you tell Bat?" I asked Agatha, eyeing her carefully. I could see the blush rising in her cheeks.

"I didn't mean to hold anything back."

Unlikely, since Agatha had never held back a juicy piece of gossip in her life. "Go on."

"Well," Agatha said, "I don't mean to speak ill of people, especially the dead, but I think I might know someone who had a motive to kill Krys Marlowe."

Chapter 4
Motive for Murder

Cheryl and I stared at Agatha with wide eyes. Someone had started a fire in the fireplace and a log popped and snapped in the sudden quiet. The flames sent eerie shadows dancing across the pale yellow walls of the kitchen and the bare windows stared back at us like giant, dark eyes. I managed to restrain a shudder at the thought that someone— maybe the killer— could be watching us from outside those windows. And Agatha had just declared she knew who it was. Maybe. Great. The killer could pounce again at any moment! If there was a killer. I had to remind myself the police hadn't ruled out food poisoning yet.

"That seems like something you might have told the police," I finally blurted.

"You shouldn't hide things like that from Bat," Cheryl agreed, sipping at her whisky in a delicate, ladylike fashion.

"Well, I don't actually know anything," Agatha admitted, taking another healthy swallow of whisky. "I just suspect."

"Spill it," I ordered, swirling my own whisky and wishing it was blackberry bourbon.

Agatha sighed. "I think I need cake to shore me up." She got up from the table and bustled around the kitchen, returning with three small dessert plates and a very large carrot cake smothered in cream cheese frosting. I nearly moaned in delight. "Picked it up at the bakery this afternoon. Can't let it go to waste." She sat down and served us each a sizeable chunk of cake.

I took a bite. Bliss. Absolute bliss.

Cheryl stared at her slice as if it might bite.

"What's wrong?" I whispered.

"I don't really care for carrot cake," she whispered back.

I snorted. "I'll be happy to eat it for you." I took another big bite and gave her a cheeky grin. More for me!

Once my mouth was empty, I waved at Agatha. "Continue. What do you suspect?"

Agatha swallowed her own bite of cake. "Well, you know that Krys worked down at Dr. Voss's office?"

"Mark Voss? The undertaker's brother?" I asked. Like most small towns, Astoria was a bit of a Gordeon knot with half the town being related to the other half of the town. It had come as little surprise to discover the undertaker and the doctor were brothers. The discovery that their sister was the local butcher had been slightly more disturbing.

Cheryl and Agatha both nodded. They'd both lived here in Astoria all their lives. I was a relative newcomer, having grown up in Portland and moved to Astoria just a few years ago. I liked the peace and quiet, the inspirational surroundings, and the wacky denizens of the small town. It made great fodder for my novels.

"That's right," Agatha said around another bite of cake. "Been working at the clinic about a year. It's just her, the doc, and that Kent girl."

"Alison," Cheryl supplied, a bite of cake held aloft on her fork. "The receptionist."

"Okay, so you think one of them could have killed Krys? But who? And how? And why?"

"Well, that's the thing. I'm not sure," Agatha admitted. "I have no idea the how. I mean she dropped dead here. I'm certain none of us did it, but nobody else was here. Unless someone snuck in..."

"Who, Agatha? Who do you suspect?"

"See, about a week ago, I was chatting to Krys over the fence—she was supervising her gardening people—and she said something that stuck with me."

"What!" Cheryl and I both all but screamed.

"She said that she knew some things that were 'going on down at that clinic.' When I asked her what, she just gave me this smirk. Kind of taunting and superior." Agatha sounded disgusted.

Krys had probably felt smug because she knew something Agatha didn't. Believe me, that was a Herculean task all on its own.

"Did you ask her what she knew?" I prompted.

"Of course I did, but she refused to say anything more about it. Only that whatever it was, it was going to make her a rich woman."

Cheryl and I exchanged glances.

"You thinking what I'm thinking?" Cheryl asked.

I nodded, certain we were on the same page. "I'm thinking blackmail."

# # #

"The question is, of course, who was Krys Marlowe blackmailing?" I was sitting in Baked Alaska overlooking the surging blue-gray waters of the Columbia River enjoying a shawarma pizza. It was piled high with spiced chicken, grilled vegetables, and dripped with tahini sauce. It was, in a word, delicious.

Baked Alaska was one of those sort of restaurants that aims for upscale rustic. In this case, they hit the mark. Rough beams of native Douglas fir soared above while highly polished broad boards of the same wood spread beneath our feet. Each table was graced with the warm glow of a hurricane lantern as the light outside was quickly fading despite the early hour. It was the perfect cross between romantic and casual.

Lucas Salvatore, my pretty-much-boyfriend, was sitting across from me with a plate full of scrumptious looking prawns. Too bad I was allergic or I'd have snagged one. He'd driven down from Portland the day after the murder to take me out to dinner. He'd claimed it was impulse, but my guess was that since he pretty much jumped in the car the minute I told him about the murder—if it was a murder—it was more about him trying to keep me out of trouble than anything. Which was, of course, ridiculous. I was perfectly capable of handling myself.

"Is that the question?" Lucas asked carefully. He was looking rather delicious in worn blue jeans and a green button down shirt that brought out the gray of his eyes. I swear his lips looked more luscious every time I saw him. I gave myself a mental shake. I needed to focus, not start mooning over Lucas. Although since we were dating, mooning over him was probably a prerequisite.

"There were only two other people working at the clinic," I plowed on, ignoring him. Nobody was raining on my parade, no matter how good looking or luscious lipped. "Dr. Voss is the obvious choice."

Lucas raised an eyebrow. "Really? Why's that?"

"Because he makes the most money," I said. "Plenty of blackmail opportunity. She could bleed him dry for years. Plus, he's kind of a jerk." I'd only met him once, right after I moved to Astoria. I'd had all my records transferred to his office, figuring that seeing a local doctor made more sense than running to Portland every time I needed a check-up. I'd found him to be arrogant and self-absorbed, willing to blame everything from a sniffle to a papercut on my being "overweight." I was not impressed. I hadn't been back since. Instead, thanks to the sizeist jerk, I had to make the trip to Portland every time I wanted to see a doctor.

He stroked his chin thoughtfully. "And the other person?"

"Receptionist. Local girl. Never met her, but Cheryl went to school with her cousin or sister or something." It was hard to keep all the inter-relationships in Astoria straight sometimes. "I can't imagine what she'd have to hide. Plus she probably doesn't earn much. Hard to blackmail somebody who's got nothing to give you, but it's always a possibility."

"Could have family money," Lucas suggested. "Or possibly something else this Marlowe woman wanted besides money."

"See," I said, patting him on the hand, "This is why I bring you along on these investigations. You have such good input."

He raised his eyes heavenward as if praying for patience. I ignored him.

"What would it be, I wonder?" I mused.

"What would what be?" he asked around a mouthful of prawn.

"If Krys wanted something from whatsername—the receptionist—what could she do for Krys that would be worth risking jail?"

Lucas chewed thoughtfully on a prawn. "Lots of things, I imagine. She could have access to drugs."

"A receptionist in a small clinic?" I frowned. "I don't know. Wouldn't they keep the good stuff locked up? Besides, I'm pretty sure everyone uses the drug store in town."

"Well, it's all conjecture anyway. There are far too many possibilities. The only way to narrow it down is to talk to the girl. Find out more about her. And the victim."

My mood improved and I grinned like a maniac. "Great idea!"

"Oh no." It came out in a groan.

"Seriously, though, you're right. I need to confront whatsername. Get her to spill her guts."

He actually put his face in his hands and groaned. "I've prodded the monster."

"Oh, stop your whining and finish your prawns."

"Why?" He eyed me suspiciously, but popped another

prawn in his mouth. "It's too late to go interrogating some poor woman."

"I'm not. I have other plans for tonight."

He frowned. "You're not breaking into some place are you? I will not bail you out if you get arrested."

"Depends on what you mean by 'breaking in.'" I gave him a slow wink and hoped it came out sexy instead of dorky.

He stared at me for a long moment, then his eyes widened and his eyes turned all smouldery. He shoved his plate away and pulled out his wallet. "Suddenly I'm very full."

Chapter 5
Identity Theft

After a somewhat sleepless night, Lucas left early the next morning for Portland. Another signing. Or maybe it was a meeting with his agent? In any case, it was something important, which was fine with me. It meant I could investigate in peace.

My first stop was the doctor's office. It was located in a squat, gray brick building, out of keeping with the cuteness overload that was Astoria's famous Victorian architecture. The small parking lot in back was empty, which was unexpected, and the door was locked. Someone had taped a sign to the inside of the door: "Closed for Emergency."

I wondered if the "emergency" was Krys Marlowe's untimely demise, or if there was a genuine medical emergency somewhere. I was kind of guessing the former; otherwise the receptionist would probably be there manning the phones and whatnot. In any case, that meant my morning plans were bunk. I needed a Plan B.

I decided I might as well pay a visit to the Marlowe family. Express my sympathy. Of course, that required a little more forethought. I was pretty sure you were supposed to bring a casserole to a house of mourning, so I headed home to stare into my pantry and figure out a game plan.

I was nearly home when something at the side of the road caught my eye. Our mayor, Charlie Bayles, was waving like a lunatic, his blue and gold sweater vest riding up his beer belly. I pulled over and rolled down the window.

"Hello, Charlie."

"Viola. Nice to run into you." He leaned down and I caught a whiff of the peppermints he was always sucking on.

Oh, boy. What was he going to try and talk me into this time? "What can I help you with?"

"Sorry?" His thick, gray eyebrows beetled together in confusion.

"You flagged me down."

"Oh, right." His brow unfurrowed. "Will you be at the Cupcake Bake-off and Eating Contest tomorrow?"

"I told you I would be." He perked up, but I interrupted him before he could say anything. "I'm still not participating. I'll watch. I'll even eat a cupcake or two, but I am not baking and I'm not stuffing my face until I'm ill and that's final."

He crossed his arms over his chest. "You really should participate more in the community, Viola. It's for a good cause."

"Hey, I'm going to be there. I'm going to eat a cupcake, donate money. What more do you want?" He opened his mouth, but I interrupted him again. "Bye, Charlie. See you tomorrow."

A minute later I pulled into my driveway, hurried into the house, and locked the door firmly behind me. Just in case Charlie-boy got it in his head to follow me home and continue badgering me about being a cupcake eating contestant. I like cupcakes. I do not want to ruin the experience by getting sick over them.

Padding to the pantry, I threw open the door, stared at the contents. There wasn't a lot in the way of ingredients for casseroles.

I don't cook much. Not because I can't, but because I don't enjoy cooking for just myself. I'd rather go out to eat and have someone else do all the work. Especially the cleaning. I do, however, enjoy the occasional bout of baking. So, I pulled flour, sugar, vanilla, and assorted other ingredients from the pantry. Before long I'd whipped up a double batch of banana oat muffins and popped them in the oven.

I made myself a cup of coffee while I waited and sat down to write some notes. Might as well go in prepared.

On a sheet of notebook paper I wrote "Marlowe Family" in big, bold letters. Krys had spoken of her husband, Mal, with derision. Not that that meant much. Krys had derided pretty much everyone, as far as I could tell from our short acquaintance.

I wrote "Mal" on one side of the page and, below that, possible motives for murder. Inheritance and insurance were the obvious choices for a spouse. There was also the possibility that one or both of them was having an affair. Or that one or both wanted to leave the marriage. But Krys hadn't struck me as the type to mess around and tiptoe about things. She'd just up and leave and not waste time. Of course, she could have been blackmailing her own husband for some reason. I couldn't imagine what or why, but stranger things have happened.

Next I turned my attention to the estranged daughter. Krys never once mentioned the girl by name and Agatha hadn't known it either. I wasn't even sure how old she was, except she was old enough to be on her own. More or less. I wrote "daughter" on the right side of the page along with my guesses for her motives. Again, there was the money angle. Plus, her mother hadn't been very loving. Maybe she'd wanted revenge or something. Or her mother could have been stopping her from doing something. Which sounded crazy. I'd yet to meet a kid over the age of fourteen who cared what their parents thought. Unless Krys had been supporting her daughter somehow —paying for college or something—and threatened to remove her support. That could start a kerfuffle.

It was all speculation, though. I needed to meet these people. Talk to them. Find out more about their relationship with Krys. Then I could decide what their motivations might be.

The smell of banana muffins permeated the air and my stomach gave a rumble. I pulled them from the oven, perfectly done, and turned them onto the cooling rack. Good thing I made a double batch, because I had every intention of keeping half of them for myself.

I popped a bite of muffin in my mouth and moaned. It was light and fluffy, melty and moist. And oh, so sweet. Just how a muffin should be.

I tossed a dozen of the still warm muffins into a basket along with a note card expressing my sympathy, and hopped into the car. It took less than ten minutes to get to the Marlowe house. It was right next door to Agatha up on the hill.

Velma Marx, the neighbor on the other side of the Marlowe's from Agatha, was in her front yard pruning some bushes. Hazel was right. The woman was eighty if she was a day. She was a tiny little thing with a mass of curly white hair tucked under a plastic rain hood, thick-lensed classes, and a floral apron over a mauve wool coat that had seen better days.

I gave her a little wave. She waved back and got on with her pruning.

The Marlowe house was not a Victorian like most of its neighbors. Instead it was a Portland Tudor. A sort of faux Tudor style popular in the 1920s. There were a few of them in town, some of them more attractive than others. The Marlowe house had brick siding in an unfortunate shade of tomato red. The trim and faux beams were a chocolate brown. Clearly an attempt to make them appear old and weathered. It didn't work. The front door was fire engine red—which clashed badly with the brick—with a brass knocker in the shape of a lion's head dead in the center. The porch lights on either side of the door would have been more at home on a Craftsman than a Tudor and empty giant blue-green glazed pots clearly meant to contain plants seemed out of place as they crowded the narrow pathway and small stoop.

The doorbell gave a low bong as I pressed the button. There was a stirring inside. The door swung open a moment later revealing a claustrophobic foyer and a dark staircase leading to a second floor.

"Yes?"

"Mr. Marlowe?"

"Yes."

Malcom Marlowe wasn't what I expected. He was short, at least a good six inches shorter than Krys had been, skinny and kind of mousy. His dark hair was swept into a sort of old-fashioned comb over (even though he had a full head of hair and didn't need to hide anything) and his hazel eyes hid behind owlish glasses that made Velma's look modern. He was also a good ten years younger than Krys had been and wore a Star Wars t-shirt and baggy gray sweat pants. One sock was white and one was pink as if he'd mixed something red into the laundry. He blinked at me expectantly. He didn't appear to be a widower deep in mourning. He looked more like a teenage boy ready for an afternoon of gaming. I was pretty sure the orange smudge on his shirt was from Cheetos.

"Um, I'm Viola Roberts. I played bunco with your wife. I'm so sorry for your loss." I tried to put as much sympathy into my tone as I could, but it was harder than I expected. Death is a sad thing and nobody deserves to die like Krys had, but the woman had been so unpleasant, plus I'd barely known her. Dredging up an ounce of pity for her was beyond me. I did, however, feel sorry for her husband, though he didn't look terribly torn up about it.

He murmured something vague. I think it was thank you, but it could have been anything. Then he stuck the nozzle of a white bottle up his nose and inhaled. It was such an odd move, I couldn't help but stare.

"Sorry," he muttered, shoving a tissue under his nose and blowing rather loudly. It was that kind of snorkly blow that is truly disgusting. "Allergies."

"Oh, sure." It seemed late in the season for allergies, but what did I know? Maybe he was allergic to mold. I held out the basket of muffins. "I baked you some muffins. I hope you like banana oat. I figured you already had a ton of casseroles." I was babbling, but I couldn't help myself. He was making me nervous for some reason. Maybe it was his lack of mourning. Or maybe just his odd, indecisive manner.

"They smell good." His voice was tentative. "It's cold out there. You want to come in?"

"Sure. Lead the way."

As I stepped into the foyer the heat shot up about a thousand degrees. It was like a sauna inside. I subtly wiped a bead of sweat from my upper lip as I removed my coat. "Nice and warm in here," I said cheerfully.

He shrugged as he took my coat from me and tossed it over the bannister. "Something's wrong with the thermostat."

I followed him down a long, dark-paneled hall. On each panel was hung a small print in a gilt frame. It looked like someone had bought post cards of classic oils and stuck them in a cheap frame thinking it would look posh. Instead it looked sad and dingy.

The hall lead into a galley kitchen brightly lit with fluorescent tubing left over from the nineties. Sure enough, there were at least a dozen casserole dishes covered in aluminum foil or plastic wrap sitting on the orange Formica counter. Looked like enough food to feed an army for a week. I added my basket to the mix while eyeing a plate of tempting cookies. They looked like the ones from Bakeology. I wondered if Malcom would notice if I slipped a few in my purse.

"The neighbors have been very nice," he said in a quiet voice. There was little inflection to indicate if he found their intrusion annoying or not. In fact, he gave no indication of grief at all over the loss of his wife.

"It's Mal, isn't it?"

He gave a half smile and for the first time I noticed he was actually kind of cute in a geeky way. Maybe I could understand what Krys had seen in him after all. Besides someone she could boss around. "Malcom. Only Krys called me Mal." I got the feeling he hadn't liked that particular nickname.

"Okay, Malcom." I gave him a bracing smile. "I only met Krys recently, but she mentioned you several times." I didn't point out that her comments had been less than kind. Pretty much every mention of her husband had been prefaced by "that slob" or "my idiot husband."

"I bet she did," he muttered. I guess he was familiar with her thoughts about him.

"Had you and Krys been married long?" I asked.

He shrugged. "A little over a year." He looked around vaguely. "You want something to drink? I think there's coffee. Or water." He frowned. "Not sure what else. Probably tequila. Krys always kept a bottle in the freezer."

"I'd love a glass of water." It was a little early in the day for tequila and I'd already had three cups of coffee.

He dutifully pulled a glass from a cupboard and filled it at the sink. "It's strange not having her here. She was always such a presence."

That was one way of putting it. "It must be really hard on you. Don't you have any family that could come stay with you?"

"Oh, Madison is here." He stared expectantly at the kitchen doorway as if expecting Madison to suddenly make an appearance.

"Madison?"

"Krys's daughter. From her first marriage. She arrived a couple days ago for a visit."

Interesting that the daughter's arrival coincided with the mother's death. "Yes, I remember Krys saying something about it." Actually, all she'd done was complain about her daughter's laziness and lack of drive. She hadn't once mentioned the girl was visiting.

"I bet." Mal gave a harsh laugh as he handed me the glass. "Those two fought like cats and dogs." He gave a sad smile. "I almost miss it. All Maddy has done today is sulk around and ask me when I'm getting out. It's really annoying." A frown puckered between his brows and then was gone as if getting himself worked up was too much effort.

My eyes widened. "Surely you get the house."

He laughed awkwardly again. "I do. I mean, it was mine to begin with. Krys's name isn't even on the deed. Bad credit, thanks to her ex."

"Really?" Sometimes a vague prompt is better than a pointed question. Malcom spilled his guts.

"Oh, yeah, Jerry— her ex— is a real piece of work. Right before we got married we started shopping for houses and discovered this whole nightmare of debts. Turned out her ex forged her name and ran up a bunch of credit cards, defaulted on loans, and I-don't-know-what-all. So, I bought the house and put it in my name only before we got married. Otherwise we'd have never gotten a loan. Krys didn't like it much, but there wasn't any other option."

"Oh, that was smart. But surely this ex of hers got arrested?"

Malcom snorted. "He would have, except the police can't find him. Bunch of losers."

That seemed a little harsh, but I made a noise I hoped he took for agreement. "I hope you're able to take some time off work. Process all this. Taking time to grieve is important."

He shrugged. "I work from home, so it's no big deal."

He really, truly didn't seem bothered that his wife was dead. Then again, if she'd treated him anything like she'd treated everyone else, it wasn't a big surprise.

"That's lucky," I said. "What do you do?"

"It's complicated. You wouldn't understand."

I arched a brown. "Try me."

"Well, see, it has to do with computers…"

The doorbell rang and Malcom gave a heavy sigh. "Probably another neighbor with another tuna noodle casserole. I hate tuna." He tromped off toward the front of the house, leaving me to my own devices.

Before I could do so much as pull open a drawer to

snoop, a twenty-something girl stomped into the kitchen. Since she was wearing purple fuzzy slippers, the stomping was decidedly ineffectual.

She stared at me from under a tangle of ink black hair. There were raccoon circles around her eyes. Apparently no one had instructed her on the importance of removing makeup before bed. I recognized her immediately as the girl Mom and I had seen arguing with her boyfriend at Caffeinate. Interesting.

"Who are you?" Her voice was a snarl.

"Viola Roberts. I brought muffins." I pointed at the basket. "You must be Madison. So sorry about your mom."

The girl didn't answer. Instead she stomped to the muffin basket, grabbed two, and stomped out of the room, completely ignoring me. What a charming child. Like mother, like daughter.

Malcom returned to the kitchen and sure enough, he was clutching a tuna noodle casserole. "What'd I tell you," he said with a heavy sigh, setting the new casserole precariously on top of an old one.

"I just met Madison," I said, taking a sip of my water. It was lukewarm. "She's...charming."

He grimaced. "She's a rude, spoiled little brat. The only reason I haven't kicked her out of the house yet is because it would make me look like a jerk."

He was right about that. It totally would, but I'm pretty sure anyone who met Madison would understand. "I take it she's always like this, then?"

"If you mean sullen and rude, then yes. And she's

been worse since she found out her mother didn't leave her anything."

I was surprised they'd read the will already. But then Malcom probably had a copy. "Not even a life insurance policy?"

He shook his head. "She didn't have one. Well, unless you count that one-thousand dollar one the credit union gives you for free when you open an account."

"So she gets nothing?"

"Not a drop. Besides, even if Krys had left her anything, everything of value is in my name."

Well, there went one of Madison's possible motives. And really, it kind of negated Malcom's major motive, too. If everything was already in his name, there wasn't any gain from Krys's death. Unless they were getting divorced and he didn't want to share.

"Listen, thanks for stopping by," Malcom said, "but I've got to get back to work."

As he showed me to the door I asked, "Did you ever meet the people she worked with?"

"You mean the doc and that girl that answered the phones? No. Didn't see the point. Why?"

"Just curious. I really am sorry for your loss."

As I walked to my car, I pondered the situation. The Marlowe family wasn't out of the woods yet. Money might no longer be an obvious motive, but there were plenty of other reasons to kill someone besides money. I just needed to dig deeper. Not to mention I now had a new suspect: Krys's ex-husband, Jerry. What better reason to kill someone than they're about to expose your fraud?

Chapter 6
Motivations Galore

On the way home I decided to try my luck at the doctor's office again. Sure enough, I spotted a twenty-year-old Honda parked at the edge of the lot in a space marked "employees." I was guessing it belonged to the receptionist because the paint was scraped, a wheel cover was missing, one of the doors was half rusted, and the antenna had a tennis ball on it for some inexplicable reason. It did not strike me as the vehicle of a doctor, even one with a small town practice.

I pulled into a spot near the door and braced myself by swiping on an extra coat of lip gloss. I eyed myself in the mirror. Looking good. I gave myself an approving nod before climbing out of the car and zipping up my jacket.

Inside, the small office was chilled to ice box temperatures despite the tiny space heater chugging away in the corner. The flooring was cheap, indoor/outdoor carpeting in an unfortunate shade of brown. The walls, once a pale blue, were now scuffed and splattered with goodness-knew-what. Two walls were lined with basic waiting room chairs in cracked powder-blue vinyl and a magazine rack held dog-eared copies of ten-year-old Better Homes & Gardens magazines. The reception desk was one of those metal and faux wood monstrosities right out of the 1980s. I half expected to hear Dolly Parton singing "Nine to Five."

There was no one behind the desk, so I took a

moment to snoop. Subtly, of course.

Other than a small "Word of the Day" desk calendar and a black plastic cup holding various pens and pencils, the desk was immaculate. The computer was even signed off, a login screen staring back at me balefully. Footsteps sounded in the hall, so I darted around to the front of the desk and made myself look as innocent as possible.

"Oh." The woman who appeared in the doorway to the reception room clutched a cup of coffee in one hand and a brand new copy of Archaeology magazine in the other. Her blonde hair was swept up in a messy bun on the top of her head. She stared at me with round, unblinking blue eyes and cupid bow lips shaped in a perfect circle of surprise. Her black, pencil skirt stopped about mid-thigh and her cheap, pink blouse flashed an ample amount of cleavage despite the fuzzy black cardigan she wore over it.

I gave her a cheery smile. "Good morning."

"I'm sorry," she said, sliding gracefully into the seat behind the desk and setting the magazine neatly to the side. "I didn't realize anyone was here. I hope you haven't been waiting long." She had a nice, well-modulated voice which probably sounded great on the phone.

"No. Not long," I assured her.

She tapped away at her computer, barely glancing at me. "Did you have an appointment?" She looked up at me expectantly.

"No," I admitted. "I was just hoping to have a quick word with the doctor. It won't take but a minute."

"I'm sorry. He isn't in today, but if you want to make

an appointment…"

"I don't need one actually. I want to speak to him about a personal matter." I handed her my card with a slight flourish.

"Viola Roberts. Author. Oh, how interesting. What do you write?"

"Historical romances."

"Neat. I don't read much fiction."

I glanced at her magazine which was opened to an article on "Ten Items Found in an Egyptian Tomb." "Well, we can't all be perfect." I laughed awkwardly as she stared at me with a blank expression. "Do you know when Doctor Voss will return?"

She shrugged and tapped a bit more at her keyboard. "Not really. You see, we lost one of our own recently." She sighed tragically, giving a little flutter of her lashes as if to emphasis the point.

"Yes. I know. Krys Marlowe. I was the one who found her, ah, body."

"You were?" That got her attention. "How awful."

"Yes, it was. Quite a shock. And that's why I wanted to see the doctor."

Her expression cleared. "For some Xanax or something?"

"No. No, I don't think I need any of that. Coffee is my drug of choice." Another blank stare, so I rushed on. "See, I also wanted to talk to you. Sorry, what was your name?"

"Alison. Alison Kent."

We shook hands. Hers was chilly and felt like a dead

fish. "Nice to meet you Alison." I decided to go for the jugular. "See, word has it that Krys Marlowe was blackmailing you."

She went sheet white and her entire body tensed up like a board. "That's not true." It came out as a whisper.

"Sure it is," I said in a bracing tone. "I have it on good authority."

"Who told you?"

"Someone very trustworthy." No way was I admitting it was Agatha. Everyone in town knew she was an incorrigible gossip.

"I didn't kill her."

"I assume you have an alibi?"

She seemed to shrink into herself. "I was with my boyfriend that night. He lives down in Seaside."

"Not a great alibi." Although actually it was, if it were true. Seaside was a good thirty-minute drive down the coast. And that was with no traffic and pushing the speed limit. Okay, breaking the speed limit.

"Why isn't it?" she wailed.

"Because he's your boyfriend. He could lie for you."

"But I was there. I swear. What do I do?"

"You tell me the truth about the blackmail, and I'll put in a good word for you with the police." I knew I had her.

Her eyes widened again and she leaned forward eagerly. "You can do that?"

"Sure. Bat and I are great friends." Which was more than stretching the truth, but Alison didn't have to know that.

"Fine." Her tone was sullen. "But you can't tell anyone. Promise?"

"Promise." I had my fingers firmly crossed behind my back. If her information solved the case, I'd have to tell Bat at the very least.

"Okay." She glanced around as if someone might be hiding behind the fake fichus. "See, I don't get paid very well."

"No, I imagine not."

"And Dr. Voss expects me to run all these stupid errands for him. Like get his dry cleaning and get new bottles of bourbon from the liquor store. Only he won't reimburse me for gas."

"Well, that's not right."

"No," she agreed. "It isn't. It's terrible. I can't afford all that extra gas. Gas is expensive, you know."

I gave a knowing nod. She wasn't wrong about that.

"So, every once in a while, I take money from petty cash. It's easy enough to fake a receipt and Dr. Voss never checks. So, you know, just five dollars here or there. Otherwise I wouldn't have enough money for gas for all his stupid errands."

"I totally get it." I perched on the edge of one of the chairs near her desk. "Absolutely understandable. I'm sure any reasonable person would agree. I mean, the man should be reimbursing you anyway."

"Well, stupid Krys Marlowe wasn't reasonable. One day she caught me taking a couple bucks from the box and sticking them in my purse. She threatened to tell the doctor. Get me fired. I begged her not to."

"I'm guessing that's when she offered to keep her mouth shut. For a price."

Alison nodded emphatically. "Only not for money. Obviously I don't have any."

"What did she want?"

"It's sooo embarrassing."

"It'll be better if you share it. Get the weight off, you know?" I wasn't sure that was true, but what the heck. We were on a roll.

"Maybe..." She mulled it over. "Here's the thing, she wanted me to try and trick her husband into bed." Alison flushed so red I thought she might be having a stroke.

"A honey trap?" I hadn't seen that one coming.

"Yeah. I think she wanted a divorce, but everything was in his name so she wanted to make sure she had something juicy to force him to give her money or something."

"Did it work?"

"Nope." A blond tendril escaped from her bun. She shoved it back with irritation. "I guess I'm not a good actress. Or maybe he's just really into his mistress."

"His mistress?" Oh, this was getting juicy! I guess my speculations hadn't been that far off after all.

"Yeah. See, when I failed to trap him, Krys got really mad. Threatened to turn me into the cops. So, I offered to sort of follow him. Like a private investigator. I mean, I've seen those cop shows on TV. It can't be that hard, right?"

That was my philosophy. "And did you?"

She nodded. "Absolutely. Found out that three times a

week he heads over to that dump of a motel up the highway. You know the one with the faded fir tree on the sign?"

I nodded. I knew the one. The Fir Lodge wasn't nearly as exciting as it sounded. It wasn't a lodge at all but a typical cheap motel that was known to rent rooms by the hour when the occasion warranted.

"Well, he meets a woman there. I don't know her name or anything, but she's short and has red hair and massive..." she held her hands in front of her chest. "You know."

"Yes. I see. Did you tell Krys?"

"Sure I did."

"When?" I asked.

Alison smiled grimly. "Two days before she died.

Shéa MacLeod

Chapter 7
Nebbiolo Noon

As usual, my friend Nina Driver was perched behind the bar at her wine shop, Sip. It was a chilly evening and she was wearing a '60s style charcoal-gray tweed shift dress with knee-high black boots. Her golden hair, usually worn around her shoulders, was done up in a sort of beehive thing. Very retro.

At the end of the bar, Lloyd— one of the local characters— sat hunched over in his usual spot. A nearly empty bottle of inexpensive red wine sat in front of him. He stared morosely at his nearly full glass, one hand shoved up into his wild, white hair.

"Hi, Lloyd," I said, giving him a little wave as I walked passed him.

He looked up, gave me a half smile, and buried his nose in his glass.

Sip was one of those cozy sorts of places with warm, red walls and racks filled with bottles of wine for purchase. You could also meet friends for a glass of your favorite vino at the bar while you watched the world go by outside. Regulars became friends in a place like Sip. I slid onto a barstool and Nina shoved a wine list at me. Not that I needed one.

"I'll have the Nebbiolo." I scooted the list back with my forefinger. The cool weather called for a warming red. "The place looks nice." Nina had wrapped the pillars with icicle shaped twinkle lights, giving the place a festive winter feel.

"Good choice. And thanks." Nina reached beneath the bar for a bottle and poured me a glass of the dark red wine. "Have you heard from Portia lately?"

"She emailed a couple of days ago. Costa Rica is agreeing with her. She's met a man down there. Sounds like they're having fun." Portia was a friend of ours who'd gotten messed up in a murder. She'd recently taken an extended vacation to recuperate.

"Well, good luck to her. Where's your partner in crime?" she asked as she slid the glass over.

"Cheryl? She's meeting me here. I think she needs to get out of the house. She's been with her mom all day."

"Charlene still freaked out about the murder?"

I nodded. "Not that I blame her. It was shocking."

Nina snorted. "That woman is a delicate flower."

Not exactly how I'd describe Charlene. Sensitive maybe, but not exactly a wilting daisy. "Well, murder will do that to you." The first sip was bliss. Warming and delicious with just a touch of jammy fruit. Just what I needed.

"Like anyone gives a flying hoo-hah that Marlowe woman got bumped off. Nasty piece of work." Nina stuck the bottle of Nebbiolo back with the rest.

I perked up. "Really? What have you heard?"

"It's not what I've heard. It's what I've experienced. Did you know she was in here the other day, drenched in perfume, and bragging about how she had a 'great nose' for wine?" Nina huffed in annoyance.

Anyone who really knows wine will tell you that the

last thing you do is douse yourself in scent before drinking it. Especially if you plan to be in public. For one thing, it wrecks your own taste. For another, it'll destroy the tasting ability of everyone around you. Not to mention that it's gross anyway. Nobody wants to have an allergy attack because you're overly fond of spritzing. Nina had a particularly sensitive nose and any kind of scent drove her nuts.

"Sounds like a pain in the butt," I agreed. "She wasn't the most pleasant person at bunco, believe me. She totally insulted Agatha's pumpkin collection."

"I bet that went over like a lead balloon."

"Oh, Agatha was not amused."

"Who do you think did it?" Nina asked. She picked up a cloth and began polishing glasses.

"Well, the police haven't confirmed it's murder yet, but I'm betting it is. I mean, people don't just drop dead of food poisoning like that." I leaned forward. "Her current husband, Mal, told me her ex-husband, Jerry, stole Krys's identity. Racked up all kinds of debts. Maybe he killed her."

"That's more a motive for her to kill him," Nina disagreed. "Maybe he killed her to prevent her from having him arrested or whatever."

"Too late. She already reported it, but the police can't find him. He's in the wind."

She shrugged. "So, what would be the point in him killing her?"

"To prevent her from testifying if it ever comes to trial," I suggested.

"I suppose." She held a glass up to the light, frowned at a smudge I couldn't see, and continued polishing. "But why bother to come back here if he's on the lam? Why not just keep going to Mexico or something?"

She had a point there. "I don't know. Hey, did you know she was blackmailing the poor receptionist down at Dr. Voss's office?" I felt only a small twinge of guilt for breaking my promise not to tell. I was solving a murder here.

"For what? He pays that kid peanuts."

"Apparently Krys roped Alison into helping her try to prove her husband's infidelity."

Nina snorted. "Everyone in town knows that man's a dog."

"Really? Mal? But he seemed so...not sexy."

"What can I say? There's no accounting for taste. But you can ask Agatha. Right after the Marlowes first moved to town, he was getting it on with Sandra Voss."

That was a surprise. "The doctor's ex-wife?"

"The very same."

"Bet the doc was thrilled about that."

Nina laughed. "They had a knockdown, drag-out fight in the Dirty Dog parking lot."

The Dirty Dog was a brew pub down near the waterfront. What it lacked in charm it made up for in good food and cheap beer.

"Who's Mal seeing now?"

Before she could answer the door swung open and Cheryl walked in. She looked a little harried, her hair standing up more than usual. She all but threw herself on the barstool next to me. "Cab. And make it a big one."

Nina eyed her carefully, but obediently poured her a glass of cabernet. The usual size. She slid it across the bar and Cheryl gulped it down. "I needed that."

"Rough time at mom's house?" I asked sympathetically. Charlene was nothing like my mother. She was warm, loving, and comforting where mine was flamboyant, dramatic, and apt to bouts of unfortunate matchmaking.

"She's just a little worked up is all. She didn't even know that Marlowe woman, yet she insisted on baking half a dozen tuna noodle casseroles to take over."

Malcom was going to love that. "Well, it's very sweet of her."

"Yeah. If only she would stop crying every five minutes." Cheryl took another gulp of wine. "What's been going on here? Any good gossip? Please tell me some good gossip."

"Nina was telling me about Malcom Marlowe's indiscretions. I just asked her who he was seeing now when you walked in," I said.

Cheryl's eyes widened. "He's a cheater pants? I should have known. Men!" Cheryl, poor thing, hadn't had very good luck with men. Duke hadn't helped with that, either. Maybe if she gave Bat a chance. "Do you suppose," she said, leaning in toward me, "that's why he killed her?"

"His wife?" Nina asked. "Why would he do that?" She began stacking the newly polished wine glasses carefully behind the counter.

"To get her out of the way, of course," Cheryl said

smugly. She gave me the eye. "You're not the only one who can solve a mystery."

I was starting to think she'd had a little too much to drink. Usually, Cheryl was the one running from an investigation.

"It's a possibility," I admitted. "But we've got to look at this from all angles. Like is Alison telling the truth about him seeing someone?"

"He definitely was," Nina assured us. "He was in here last week with a red-head. They seemed very chummy. Kinda dangerous seeing her right out in the open like that at a place his wife might see. Not too bright."

That jived with what Alison had said. "Did you know her?" I asked.

"Never seen her before," Nina said. "But they were definitely more than friends."

"I'm betting it's the same woman Alison Kent saw him with at that bump and grind motel just out of town."

Nina's eyes lit up. "Oh, scandal!"

"Too bad we don't know who she is," Cheryl said mournfully.

"Diana Landford."

We all turned to stare at Lloyd. He just kept gazing down at his wine glass.

"What was that, Lloyd?" Nina prodded, cocking her head to one side.

He finally glanced up, his long face permanently set in a hang-dog expression. "I saw 'em that night they were in here. Recognized her immediately. She's a real estate agent down south."

Cheryl frowned. "What? Like California?"

"Nah. Lincoln City. My brother bought a house through her." We all stared at Lloyd as he drained his glass and tossed a few bills on the counter. Then he walked out, his nearly empty bottle tucked under one arm, without saying another word.

"Well. Once again Lloyd proves a deft hand at gossip," Nina said.

"Guess I need to go track down Diana Landford," I said. "Because she's got a very good motive for murder."

.

Chapter 8
The Problem With Escapees

The day of the Cupcake Bake-Off and Eating Contest dawned bright and chilly. I decided the best move at the moment, since I didn't have time to drive over two hours down the coast to Lincoln City, was to confront Malcom about his cheating ways. Maybe he would reveal more about his relationship with Diana Landford. Maybe he'd slip up and admit he, or Diana, killed Krys. Yeah, hope springs eternal. More than likely he'd toss me out on my backside even though he was about half my size.

The Marlowe house looked exactly as it had the day before. Only instead of birds chirping and wind chimes jangling, I could hear shouting and screaming from inside the house. It was too muffled to make out the nature of the argument, but I was pretty sure Malcom and his step-daughter were having one heck of a dust up. And I wanted to know why.

Apparently so did Velma, since she was out on her porch in a pink housecoat glaring at the Marlowe house. She didn't even notice me as I crept around the side of the house to where a living room window stood open a crack. I wasn't sure if they'd forgotten it was open or if they really just wanted a tiny sliver of fresh air thanks to the jungle temperatures inside. In any case, it suited my purposes. I could make out the voices much better.

"…you owe me you little…" That was Malcom. And the word he called Madison was not a very nice one.

Madison screamed something unintelligible followed by, "Try and stop me." That was followed by another unrepeatable moniker.

There was a scuffle. Something crashed followed by more screaming.

"I'll report your ass to the cops." Madison this time.

"Oh, just try it, little miss thing. I'll tell them exactly what you did to your mother."

There was a pause, followed by the crack of flesh hitting flesh, followed by Malcom screaming a long string of cuss words. If I had to guess, I'd say Madison just smacked him across the face. I wasn't sure if I should cheer or call the cops on both of them. Instead, I slipped back to the front of the house, narrowly avoiding the world's largest cobweb, and leaned on the doorbell.

The door flung open and a red-faced Malcom stood there. Today he was wearing a Doctor Who t-shirt and black sweat pants. "What do you…? Oh, Miss Roberts. Can I help you?" He gave me a big, fat, fake smile.

"Oh, you know, I was just in the area. Thought I'd stop by and see how things were going. See if you need anything." I gave him a perky smile.

"Thanks. That's very kind, but I'm alright." He started to close the door, but I put my hand on it, stopping him.

"You sure? Because I thought I heard screaming." I peered around him, trying to get a better glimpse into the house. Nothing appeared out of place and I couldn't see the living room from this angle. Darn it.

Malcom very carefully edge to the side, barring my way. "No. No. Just a misunderstanding. Everything is fine." He gave me a tight smile. "Truly. Thanks for stopping by…"

"You know, I had a quick question for you." I leaned casually against the doorjamb, further preventing him from closing the door. "Just this funny thing I heard in town."

"Oh?" He lifted an eyebrow, but otherwise appeared uninterested.

"Yeah. Word has it you've been real chummy with that real estate agent out of Lincoln City. What's her name?" I tapped my chin as if thinking. "Diana. Landford. Interesting. You didn't mention that before."

He dropped the fake smile, glaring at me. "Because it's none of your business."

"No," I agreed. "But Detective Battersea and I are real good friends and I bet he'd be interested." I chuckled a little as if delighted with myself.

Malcom leaned forward, fury written in every line of his face. Clearly he was not amused. "Butt out, Miss Roberts, or you'll regret it." And with that he slammed the door on his face, nearly taking off my nose in the process.

"Well, that was rude," I said at the closed door.

"Ignore him. He's in a foul mood."

I turned in time to see Madison come around the corner of the house dragging a black wheeled suitcase. She was dressed all in black, including her puffy coat, but I got the strong feeling it wasn't for the purpose of mourning.

"Did you know about his affair?" I asked. I figured

blunt was the way to go with Madison. She seemed to appreciate it.

"Sure," she admitted. "Just about everybody did including my mother. Can't blame him either. Mom was a jerk to him. Cheated on him from the beginning. With total losers, too." She frowned. "Not that Mal is such a catch."

"Did he know?" I asked, surprised. "That your mother knew about his affair, I mean?"

She shrugged and checked her phone. "Who knows? Who cares?" Clearly she didn't. She dragged her suitcase to the curb and stood there looking bored.

"Going somewhere?" I asked.

"Anywhere but here."

"Where will you stay?" If Malcom owned everything and Madison didn't have a job, I couldn't imagine her finding a decent, safe place.

"It's not a problem. Malcom may have had everything in his name, but he couldn't control her life insurance policy."

That surprised me based on the information I'd been given. "Malcom said she didn't have one."

Madison snorted. "She's had one since I was a kid. I'm surprised she was still paying on it, but she was, and it was still in my name. Shocker. So I'll be fine. There's my ride." She nodded toward the silver car that had just pulled up to the curb, one of those ride share stickers in the window.

"You should probably stay in town," I called to her as the driver stowed her suitcase in the trunk. "You know, in case the police have questions."

"The police can suck it." She hopped in the car and the car took off with a screech.

I stared after it. So now Madison was back on the table as a suspect. Her mother's death was her monetary gain. But then, Malcom and Diana also had motives. Malcom could have killed Krys, either to get rid of her so he could be with Diana, or because he found out Krys was cheating and got angry. In my experience, just because one person in a couple is cheating doesn't mean he or she is okay with the other person cheating. Or Diana could have killed Krys to free up Malcom. Wouldn't be the first time a mistress bumped off a wife. So many possibilities.

But the one thing I had to do straightaway was call Bat and let him know one of the prime murder suspects was about to leave town.

# # #

"Seriously, Viola, you called to tell me that?" Bat sounded annoyed.

"Well, I thought you'd want to know. I mean, Madison does benefit from Krys's death. And now she's running away. Don't you find that the tiniest bit suspicious?" I asked. I had the speaker phone on in the car as I headed down the hill to the school gym where the Cupcake Bake-Off and Eating Contest was to take place. Charlie would skin me alive if I wasn't there.

Bat gave a heavy sigh. "Not at all. Her step-father is a jerk. She probably just wanted to get away from him. Stay with her boyfriend."

"You know him?"

"Jake? Sure. Good kid."

I wondered if Jake was the same kid I'd seen Madison arguing with in the coffee shop. "Is he blond?" I described the boy I'd seen Madison with.

"Sounds like Jake. Why?"

"Just curious." I wasn't sure if their argument was important or not, but I filed it away for the future, just in case. "I thought you'd be a little more interested. She's a prime suspect."

"I wouldn't say prime."

"What would you say?"

"We don't even know it's a murder, Viola. We're still waiting on the coroner's report."

"Come on. I'll take anything."

I could almost see him rolling his eyes. "I can't comment on an ongoing investigation."

"Oh, sure, pull that card now."

"Is that all?" Now he was being nasty.

"Yes," I snapped back. "That's all. Though maybe if you're not going to take this seriously, I should inform the mayor."

"Do what you must." And with that he hung up.

I shot a glare at the phone. Well, he might not be taking this seriously, but I was. And little miss snippy pants was at the top of my list. Right after cheater-pants Malcom and his bit on the side. Yep, I had a nice healthy suspect list and I was going to prove to Bat that one of them was the killer. But first, I needed to have a chat with

Jake. I wanted to know more about that argument he'd had with Madison.

# # #

Jake Bayles was surprisingly easy to find. He was, after all, the mayor's son. All I had to do was ring up Agatha and ask her where the kid hung out. Turned out he worked part time at Poe's, the larger of the two local bookstores.

Poe's was one of those places that belongs firmly in the past, but somehow clings to life despite the appearance of big box bookstores and online shopping. The lighting was dim, the ceiling low, and the floor space crowded with bookshelves crammed to overflowing with both new and used tomes. A long counter tripled as checkout, display, and coffee bar. The scent of old books mingled with fresh brewed coffee, tickling the nose with its pleasant fragrance and the mind with memories.

In the corner near the door, a raggedly dressed man with bleary eyes sat drinking a plain cup of coffee and talking loudly in a slurred voice. The stench of unbathed body and unwashed clothes warred with the more pleasant scents of the shop. The thirty-something blonde woman behind the counter broke off conversation long enough to give me a smile and welcome. I'd seen her on previous visits though for the life of me I couldn't remember her name. People really ought to wear nametags.

"I'm looking for Jake," I said, returning her smile and

trying to ignore the fact that the drunk was leering at me. I had no idea what he found so interesting. I was wearing plain old jeans with an ultramarine sweater and gray ankle high boots. No cleavage or bare anything. Maybe his drunken state had something to do with it.

"Jake's in the back, shelving." She pointed to the back corner of the store where I knew from experience they kept the cookbooks. I love cookbooks. Especially ones with nice photography. I have a ridiculously huge collection of Nigella and Barefoot Contessa books. I've never cooked a single thing from them, but I love the pictures of food.

I made my way through the crowded shop, squeezing past piles of books, until I found Jake standing on a step ladder, cramming cook books willy-nilly onto shelves. I doubted he was even bothering with alphabetizing.

"Hey, Jake."

He turned around. Sure enough it was the boy I'd seen arguing with Madison. Today he was wearing jeans, black Chuck Taylors, and a gray t-shirt featuring some band I'd never heard of. "Who are you?"

"Viola Roberts. I'm an author."

"If you want to feature your book or something you gotta talk to the owner. He'll be in after lunch." He turned back to his work.

"Actually, I wanted to talk to you. I have a couple questions."

He frowned. "About what?"

"About you and Madison Marlowe."

His brow furrowed in confusion, then his expression

cleared. "You mean Madison Enthwaite."

"Enthwaite?"

"Yeah. Her real dad's name. She refused to use her stepdad's name and it pissed her mom off no end."

Well, that made sense. Especially since Malcom and Madison couldn't stand each other. "Right. So, you and Madison are dating?"

He shrugged, sagging back to lean against the bookshelf which seemed a little precarious. "I guess. Mostly we're just hanging."

"Gotcha." Sort of. I wasn't sure what specified "hanging" to today's youth, but I was guessing it was what us "old folks" called dating. "A couple days ago I was at Caffeinate and I saw you two arguing."

His gaze shifted uneasily. "So? People argue."

"Well, it was interesting because that was the night Madison's mom died."

A muscle flexed in his jaw. "So?" he repeated stubbornly.

"Well, I happened to catch part of your argument and I know Madison was threatening to kill her mom." It was a total lie. I'd heard no such thing, but Jake went white as a sheet. I knew I had him. "It doesn't look good, Jake, you arguing with her about that and then her mom turning up dead. You could be charged as an accessory after the fact. How would that look? The mayor's son going to prison for murder."

He practically fell off the ladder, he scuttled down it so fast. "I didn't do anything." He was frantic, flailing his arms in panic. "It was just... talk. You know. Maddy was so angry. Her mom was being a bitch, and Maddy was just— you know—ranting. She didn't mean it."

"Tell me exactly what she said."

"Are you going to tell the police?"

"Tell me what she said, and maybe I won't."

He shrugged. "It was just the usual, you know. Her mom was always pulling something. Going through her stuff, breaking into her computer, trying to get her money. I can't even remember what happened that morning, but Maddy was super pissed and was all like 'I've had it. That's the last straw. I'm going to ring her neck.' You know, something like that. And I'm like 'Chill. You're overreacting.' Then she gets all mad and tells me I'm a loser. So I got mad and left."

Stormed out was more like it, but I didn't bother to point out the minor discrepancy. "She said 'ring her neck.' Not 'kill her' or something?"

"No. Definitely the neck thing."

"What happened after that?"

He scrunched up his nose as if trying to remember. "I took her home. Dad was working late, so I ordered a pizza and calmed her down."

I gave him a look. "With pizza."

"Well, I might have taken some of my dad's beer." He looked worried. "You won't tell him will you?"

Charlie-boy? Not if I was dragged over hot coals. "Where did she go after the movie?"

"She didn't. She stayed the night."

Giving her an alibi. Darn it. I thanked Jake and hurried out of the bookstore. I hated to admit it, but there went one of my suspects, although I still wasn't convinced she wasn't involved somehow. I mentally crossed Madison off the list. For now.

Shéa MacLeod

Chapter 9
The Great Cupcake Bake-Off and Eating Contest

The Cupcake Bake-Off and Eating Contest was in full swing by the time I arrived at the Astoria High School gym. It looked like half the town had turned out to watch the insanity. Brightly colored balloons and streamers were draped everywhere. Children ran screaming through the halls high on sugar. It was chaos.

I paused at the table near the entrance to buy my ticket. Agatha was perched on a folding chair, cupcake shaped earrings swinging from her ear lobes. She wore a vintage-style apron covered with cupcakes over a simple cream-colored pantsuit. "Hi, Viola. Come to watch the lunacy?" Her bright red lipstick matched the "frosting" on her cupcake earrings.

"Sure." I sniffed the air which smelled sweetly of vanilla and sugar. "And to eat a cupcake or two."

"Five dollars." She took my money and stamped my hand with a cupcake-shaped stamp. "Avoid Charlie-boy if you can. He's trying to rope anyone he can into the eating contest. Hazel had to lie and tell him she's a diabetic."

I grinned. "I'll do my best. Any news about the investigation into Krys's death?"

"Why would I have news?" She batted her eyelashes.

I gave her a look.

"Fine, fine," she laughed. "Unfortunately not. But I've

got my ear to the ground."

"Let me know if you hear anything."

I drifted into the gym, wincing at the assault on my ear drums. A kid that looked about eight screamed at his parents for more cupcakes. He was already covered in frosting and crumbs and his parents were completely oblivious despite the screaming, eyes glued to their smartphones. I wandered over to the row of folding tables where the bake-off contestants had their wares for purchase. At the first table, two women I didn't recognize argued vehemently.

"I can't believe you tried to pass those off as your own. Please. Anyone would know at first bite they're from a store-bought mix," the first woman snapped.

"Clearly not everyone did," the second crowed, waving a red ribbon.

The next table over contained cupcakes of a particularly odious color. The cakes themselves were an off-putting brownish color while the frosting was weirdly chunky and baby poop green.

"Did you bake those?" I asked the teenaged boy behind the table, trying not to sound horrified.

"Naw. My dad did." He slouched against the table. "Want one?"

"What flavor are they?"

He beamed. "Oh, they're super healthy. The cupcakes are flax seed with quinoa."

"And the frosting?" I was half afraid to ask.

"Avocado. Here." He thrust one at me. "On the house."

I took a tentative bite and nearly spit it across the table. The cake wasn't so bad. If you like the flavor and texture of sawdust. The frosting, on the other hand, tasted like someone dumped sugar in the guacamole. I made my excuses and headed for the nearest garbage can to dump the hideous thing.

After ridding myself of the offending baked good, I spotted Velma at one table and hurried over. I grinned when I saw the big, blue ribbon pinned to a plate of cupcakes.

"Congratulations," I shouted over the din. "Looks like your cupcakes are the ones to try."

She smiled back, clearly thrilled over her win. "Which would you like? Chocolate cake with coconut frosting? Peanut butter cake with chocolate frosting? Or vanilla with framboise frosting?"

"How about one of each?"

I paid for the cupcakes and Velma put them in a little box for me to take home. Not that they'd get that far. I have a weakness. What can I say?

"So how'd it go?" I asked as she handed me the box. "Tell me about the bake-off."

"It was very exciting," she said, clasping her wrinkled hands together. I noticed there was cocoa powder caked beneath a couple of her fingernails. "We had one hour to bake and frost as many cupcakes as we could. Of course, some only baked one kind." She leaned over and glared down the row at a woman who had dozens of green frosted cupcakes lining her table. "But variety is always the key to winning," she finished smugly.

"I can see that."

She tilted her nose up. "I don't care what anyone says. That Marlowe woman never had a chance of winning."

It was an odd comment until I remembered what Agatha had told me on bunco night: Velma had been angry because Krys had started winning the garden contest. And she was worried Krys would win the bake-off, too. I had no idea whether or not Krys was any kind of a baker and I found it ridiculous anyone could get so worked up over a stupid cupcake contest, but that's a small town for you.

"Well, they look delicious," I assured her. "I can't wait to try one, but the cupcake-eating contest is about to start. I better go check it out." She waved goodbye as I took off into the crowd.

The cupcake-eating contest was about as you'd imagine it. Three men and a woman sat at a long table covered in black plastic bags. In front of each one was a plate of cupcakes. Charlie made a long speech about how the money raised from this event was going to help the town. Everyone looked bored. Then the contest started. Herb Alpert and the Tijuana Brass blared from the loud speakers as the contestants dove into their respective plates of cupcakes.

By the time the contest was over and the only female contestant was declared the winner, one guy had puked, one nearly passed out, and the third threw a temper tantrum— and the remaining cupcakes, splattering the onlookers with frosting.

"Quite an event, hey, Miss Roberts?" Charlie had

snuck up on me without my noticing.

"Uh, sure, Mr. Mayor."

"Just call me Charlie. Everyone does." Actually, everyone called him "Charlie-boy" behind his back. He was their mayor, and everyone in Astoria would stick up for him to outsiders… but really, they knew he was a pain in the ass. "You should really join the bake-off next year. I'm certain you could really elevate this event."

I gave him a sideways look. Elevate? "I'm not sure what you mean by that," I said dryly.

"It's a compliment," he said, with a broad smile. "Those puddings you baked at Christmas…" he kissed his fingertips.

Seriously. How many cooking shows had the man been watching lately? "Even though you ended up in the hospital?" There had been a poisoning incident which involved my Christmas puddings.

"Not your fault." He waved it off. "And you solved the mystery and prevented a murder. Besides, the puddings were delicious, minus the poison, of course. See? Elevated."

"I'm not really a bake-off kind of person."

He frowned, then I saw the lightbulb turn on. "You could still be a judge. I know you like cupcakes."

He wasn't wrong about that. "We'll talk about it," I said just to get him to shut up and leave me alone.

"Excellent! I'll call you."

Just then I saw Malcom Marlowe through the crowd, and I caught a flash of red next to him. Holy cow! He was right there in public with his mistress!

"Sorry, Charlie. I gotta go." Before the mayor could open his mouth, I was off like a shot, pushing my way through the press of people. I stepped on a cupcake and got frosting on my shoe, but I ignored it. I needed to catch Mal and his mistress. I had questions.

Unfortunately, by the time I'd got to where they'd been standing, they were gone. With a sigh, I made my way over to Agatha who was still manning her station by the door.

"Did you see Malcom Marlowe leaving just now?"

"Afraid not. In fact, I haven't seen him at all."

Maybe I was hallucinating. "Charlie-boy cornered me about next year's bake-off."

"That man has an obsession. What did you tell him?"

"I told him I'd think about it."

Her eyes widened. "Are you insane? He'll hound you into the grave."

"I didn't know what else to do. I was just trying to get him off my back."

She shook her head. "All I can say is get out of town as fast as you can. And you might want to think about changing your name."

Ah, the joys of small town living.

Chapter 10
The Problem With Bees

That evening when I got home, I did a quick internet search on Diana Landford, Malcom Marlowe's mistress. Say that three times fast.

It was easy enough to find Diana's real estate website. She appeared to be one of many one-woman shows up and down the coast. Her photo was of a young thirty-something, well-coiffed red head with a perky smile that might or might not be fake. She listed a whopping three houses on her site, which wasn't bad for a small office, but wasn't exactly going to set the world on fire. Maybe Diana wanted Krys gone so that she could marry Malcom, have a nice house and a comfortable lifestyle in Astoria. It seemed like an old fashioned, rather silly reason for murder, but I'd heard of worse. Like killing your wife because she served you cold eggs. Seriously, that really happened. I know because I watch way too many true crime shows on TV.

In any case, Diana had just as good a motive as anyone. Whether she had opportunity or not was another matter. Bat was probably checking up on that, but it wouldn't hurt to do my own digging. She might respond better to a woman. Or not. But curiosity and all that.

Further research revealed that while Diana Landford had a presence all over social media, it was strictly for business. Nothing personal. I couldn't even find her tagged in friends' photos or anything. The woman took internet security to new heights. Annoyed, I logged off the internet and opened my latest manuscript. I spent the rest of the evening lost in the

Wild West with sexy cowboys, sassy madams, and one very confused schoolmarm.

# # #

Morning came far too early, the sun managing to find its way around the tiniest openings in my bedroom blackout curtains. I scowled at nothing in particular and tried to burrow deeper under the duvet. No luck. I couldn't will myself back into dreamland. Might as well get up.

I squinted at the clock. Nine. I'd been up writing until almost three which meant a whopping six hours of sleep. Not exactly my idea of rest. I was a solid eight- to nine-hours girl, but coffee called, the day was sunny, and there was no getting around the fact that sleep was off the menu.

I wrapped myself in my worn, lavender terry cloth robe, slipped on my pink-and-white-striped slipper socks, and staggered into the kitchen. I managed to make a cup of coffee despite my eyelids being at half-mast. The aroma of brewing beans immediately sent me to my happy place. There is nothing like the scent of fresh coffee, in my book.

I was just sitting down at the kitchen table to enjoy

said cup of coffee when something buzzed near my face. Annoyed, I flicked at it. Probably a fly. It veered off, but it was back a moment later, hovering over my cup right as I was trying to take a sip. I brushed at it again, only to feel a sharp pain on my hand. I looked down to find a honey bee, its stinger firmly planted in my skin.

With a hiss, I ripped it off and plucked out the stinger. Then I grabbed an ice cube from the freezer and slapped it on the sting, cussing like a sailor the whole time. I'd been stung by bees twice before in my life, and it was never pleasant. The first time, I'd stepped on the darn thing. If you can imagine trying to walk with a bee sting in the arch of your foot, you can imagine how enjoyable it was. The second time, I was in the midst of a raging case of chicken pox. It was like adding insult to injury.

I thought it weird a bee was buzzing around my kitchen at that hour of the morning and in the winter, too. The windows and doors had been shut up, and it had rained during the night. Not exactly a time for bee central. I supposed it could have slipped in at some point on a warmer day, confused about the time of year, but it was just strange. Bees in the house weren't a common problem for me even in spring and summer.

Shrugging it off, I headed to the bathroom for ointment and a Band-Aid. Good thing I didn't have a bee allergy.

Chapter 11
Doctors and Librarians

I tried to get some work done. Really I did. But questions kept swirling in my mind about who could have killed Krys Marlowe and why. There were so many options, and I was getting nowhere. I wondered if Bat was having any luck.

Finally I decided that work would have to wait. My heart wasn't in it, and my mind was definitely wandering. So I threw on a warm jacket, grabbed my purse, and headed out.

I wasn't sure where I was going. Zero plan. That was me. But as I passed Dr. Voss's office, I saw a black Mercedes parked in one of the employee spots. I grinned to myself. Now that was the kind of car a doctor would drive. Time for Dr. Voss to face the music.

I swung into the parking lot and parked right next to the doctor's car. I tried to peer inside, but the windows were tinted and I couldn't make out much. Not that it mattered. I doubted he'd keep incriminating evidence in his car for the world to see. He'd have to be pretty dumb for that.

Inside, Alison looked like a deer in headlights when she saw me enter. I couldn't blame her. There were three other people in the waiting room and me blabbing about her secret money liberation was probably not on her morning agenda.

"Hi, Alison," I said cheerfully. "Is the doc in? I need

to have a quick word." I started around the desk, headed toward the doctor's office.

"Uh, he's with a patient." She made no move to stop me.

"Great. I'll wait in his office."

"But..." I ignored her, sailing on past and down the hall. Dr. Voss's office was easy to find. It was the one with a big brass nameplate with his name on it in enormous black letters. I frowned. He was the only doctor in the building and still he needed the world to know how important he was.

I pushed the door open slightly and peered inside. The room was empty. Alison hadn't been lying about Dr. Voss being busy. I stepped inside and closed the door after me.

The two side walls were lined with bookshelves. The back wall was covered in diplomas, awards, and pictures of what I assumed was Dr. Voss shaking hands with moderately important people. A fake fichus—to match the one in the lobby—took up one corner. And in the center of the room was a massive desk about the size of a football field.

Since I had the place to myself for a moment, I decided to poke around a bit. Voss's computer was powered up but showing the login screen. Dagnabbit. I was hoping he'd be a bit more careless. Not that I expected to find a written confession on his desktop, but you never know. I gave it an honest shot, but half a dozen password options proved fruitless.

Next I rummaged around in his desk drawers. Nothing

more interesting than several packages of HoHos and a tin of mints that smelled like they contained something more than just peppermint oil. A doctor high on marijuana while attending patients could be problematic, but would it be blackmail-worthy? Hard to tell.

The trash can was empty except for a crumpled phone message to call his mother. The bookshelves held boring medical books, just like you'd expect. My snooping was a bust.

I had just sat down in one of the visitor chairs when the door flew open. "What are you doing here?"

I turned and gave him a mild smile. "Good morning, Dr. Voss." We'd only met once before, briefly. He looked enough like his undertaker brother that they could have been twins. He was tall and angular with thinning hair and shrewd eyes. A slight pudge around the middle set him apart from his brother and gave away his love of HoHos.

"Don't play games, missy. I know why you're here." He slammed the door shut and stomped around to the other side of his desk and stood there glaring at me.

His words surprised me. How did he know I was investigating Krys Marlowe's death? Had Agatha spilled the beans? "Do you?"

"I won't pay another dime. You hear me? She's dead. You have no proof. It's my word against yours." He slapped his clipboard on the desk with a resounding thwack.

I leaned back. Interesting. I decided to play along. "Really? You think there's no proof?"

He went sheet white and thrust his forefinger in the

direction of the door. "Get out of here before I call the cops."

"And tell them what? That I'm blackmailing you? You'd have to admit you'd done something blackmail worthy. And besides, I haven't asked for a thing." I gave him a look of abject innocence. He didn't buy it.

Voss's face turned red, then purple. I was a little afraid I might need to brush up on my CPR skills any minute. "Listen, you..."

"Now, now," I with false cheer. "Careful of your blood pressure." This was sort of fun. I shouldn't be taking so much pleasure in torturing the man, but he'd clearly done something awful if he was that afraid of blackmail. Hey, I've seen Perry Mason. I know how these things work.

"Get out!" he roared.

I shrugged as I stood. "This isn't over, Dr. Voss."

"Oh, yes, it is. Get. Out." He stormed around the desk and flung open the door. I sashayed through, heading toward the front desk.

Before I exited the hall to the lobby I turned around to find him glaring after me. I gave him a little finger wave, and I swear he nearly passed out.

How interesting. What could the good doctor be hiding?

# # #

Curious beyond belief, I did a quick search on my smart phone the minute I climbed in my car. There wasn't much I found on Voss except his medical credentials, business location, and a copy of his resume on LinkedIn. His brother had far more of a social media presence, which I suppose was to be expected of an undertaker looking for business. So there wasn't much online, but there were still other ways of doing research.

I pulled out of the parking lot and drove toward the library. I could have walked; it was only a couple blocks over from the doctor's office, but I was half afraid Voss would key my car or something.

I parked behind the library— out of sight of Voss's office— and walked around to the front of the building. Sometime in the 1960s, somebody had thought it was a good idea to build a "modern" building for the public library. It was not a good idea. What resulted was, in my opinion, a jarring eyesore in an otherwise picturesque town. Instead of lovely Victorian or turn of the century architecture that peppered the town, the library was a block of cement. It was so ugly it made me cringe.

Inside at least, there were books to sooth the soul. I ignored the flickering overhead fluorescents and headed to the newspaper section. Like most newspapers these days, the local paper was all online. Just plug in a search and voila! But the paper had only jumped online about ten years ago, and they hadn't caught up to their backlog yet. My best bet was to rummage through the old papers and try to find something on Voss.

According to the sign on the doctor's door, he'd established his practice fifteen years ago. That left me five years of papers to slog through. I sighed heavily. This could take forever.

"Need help with something?" Moira Renner, one of the librarians, poked her head around the corner and peered at me through horn-rimmed glasses. Her graying dark hair had at one point in the day been pinned neatly on top of her head, but half of it was now tumbling around her shoulders. Her salmon pink cardigan clashed with her skin tone and the colors in her pink and purple floral print dress.

"Hi, Moira. Ah, yeah, I'm doing some research. For my latest book." Big fat lie. I wrote historical romances, not modern murder mysteries. Although the way things were going, I certainly had enough fodder for the latter. "I was trying to find some information on someone."

She lifted an iron gray eyebrow. "Whom?"

Oh, look at her with the proper grammar. "Doctor Voss. The online information only goes back ten years. I was hoping to find something in the five years before that."

The other eyebrow went up. "Anything specific?"

"Naw. Just anything interesting. About his practice or whatnot."

She snorted. "You want interesting? I'll give you interesting." She stalked over to the shelves, peered at the papers for a moment, and yanked a handful down. "Try these on for size." She slapped them down in front of me then disappeared around the stacks toward the front desk.

Curioser and curioser.

I opened up the oldest newspaper first, scanning it for any sign of Voss. Finally, I found a small article on page twelve about Voss being sued by a former colleague for sexual harassment. I'd have liked to say I was shocked, but nothing surprised me anymore.

The article gave little information except that Voss had worked for the Portland Medical Clinic and that one of the female employees had accused him of harassment. I was betting that was what drove Voss to open up his own practice in Astoria. No doubt he wanted to get away from the scandal. Is that what Krys had been blackmailing him over? Something that happened years ago? Unless the scandal had followed him here...

I grabbed the next paper. Again, the information was slim. More about the doctor and the good things he'd done for the community followed by a brief update on the lawsuit, quickly glossed over. It was clear that whoever wrote the article was far from impartial and, as seemed too often to be the case, Dr. Voss's privilege bought him favor with the justice system.

The last paper gave me the goods. The lawsuit had been settled out of court. Details were sketchy, but it gave me one thing. The name of the woman who'd sued the good doctor: Krys Marlowe.

.

Chapter 12
The Ugly Past

"What was Krys Marlowe doing working for the man she sued fifteen years ago?" Cheryl asked as she took a bite of a giant lemon poppy seed muffin. "Personally, I'd have stayed as far away from that snake as I could get."

"Good question. Unfortunately, Krys is dead and Voss was pretty close-mouthed when I confronted him earlier." We were sitting in Bakeology, the local bakery and coffee shop, drinking coffee, munching baked goods, and pretending to write. Somebody had tuned Pandora to an old-school jazz station. I approved.

"Did you ask him about the lawsuit?" Cheryl asked.

I swallowed the last bit of cherry chocolate scone. "Unfortunately, I hadn't found out that juicy little tidbit at the time, but you'd better believe I'm going to be asking about that next time I see him."

"Don't you think it's weird, though? Working for the man who sexually harassed you and then you sued for it?" Cheryl chewed on a bit of her muffin. "I mean, how awkward would that be?"

"Even weirder that he'd hire the woman that sued him. You'd think he would have sent her packing the minute she walked through his front door."

"Exactly." Cheryl nodded. "People are weird." She took another bite of muffin and moaned. "These things are like crack."

She wasn't kidding. "You should try the chocolate

cherry scones. You will pass out from the sheer deliciousness."

"I'm totally trying that next."

Sandy, owner of Bakeology and baker of said glorious muffins and scones, was touched by magic. I was convinced of it. Her baked goods were out of this world and totally addictive. But we were getting sidetracked.

"Anyway," I continued. "I want to find out more about Krys Marlowe before she came to Astoria. I think there's something there."

"Something besides her being a very unpleasant person, you mean?"

"Well, that," I admitted, "but I think there must be something else to it. I don't know what. But there have got to be skeletons in the closet of a person like that."

"Lots of them, no doubt." Cheryl stood up. "I'm getting a scone. Want anything?"

"Another caramel latte wouldn't go to waste."

"Coming right up."

As Cheryl trotted off to get our refreshments, I turned to stare out the large front window. Cars flashed by in either direction. Traffic was slowing down as winter set in, but plenty of Portlanders still escaped the city on weekends to relax and unwind on the coast. A barge sailed by out in the bay, crossing beneath Astoria Bridge on its way into the port. Seagulls wheeled and dove, no doubt spotting tasty treats. And someone stared back at me, mouth hanging open in surprise.

"Madison?"

She couldn't have heard me from the other side of the

window, but she turned and ran off, like she'd seen a ghost. Cheryl was right. People were weird.

"Okay, so I was doing some research of my own." Cheryl's voice interrupted my thoughts as she set a coffee cup in front of me. She sat down and began to munch her scone. How she ate so much and stayed so thin was beyond me.

"What sort of research?" I asked.

"On our victim, of course."

"Shh. Lower your voice." I glanced around to make sure no one was listening. No one was. The barista was busy foaming milk and making a god-awful racket. Nearby a twenty-something boy was hunched over his laptop wearing a pair of enormous headphones. The only other person was an old man on the other side of the bakery with his nose in a newspaper and a sandwich clutched in one gnarled hand. I realized with a start it was Lloyd from Sip. Boy, he sure got around.

"Why?" Cheryl asked around her scone. "You think somebody's gonna think we're killers or something?" She sounded doubtful. In truth, I was more afraid word would get back to Detective Battersea that I was investigating again.

"No. I just think we should be careful."

She shrugged. "Fine. Whatever. Do you want to hear what I found out or not?"

"Sure."

She leaned forward, excitement on her face. "So. I was doing a little research online. I couldn't figure out why Krys Marlowe would come to a small town like Astoria. I mean, she had 'city girl' written all over her. So I figured something must have happened to bring her out here."

"Good point. And?"

"And, two years ago, Krys was involved in a hit and run. Somebody died."

My eyes widened. "She killed someone?"

"I'm not sure she was driving, but she was involved somehow," Cheryl said. "A car hit a kid. Never came out of his coma. Eventually the kid died."

That was horrible. "Why wasn't she in jail?"

"That's the thing. I'm not sure. The article didn't say and I couldn't find out much more on it. But I did get the name of the journalist who wrote the story. I thought you might want in on the questioning."

She knew me well.

# # #

The woman who strode into The Prohibition was not what I expected from a journalist. She was about fifty, give or take five years. Her hair was that odd sort of bluish gray hair that was so in vogue these days, cropped close to the skull so it stood up randomly like a startled chicken. She wore skinny jeans, knee-high purple Doc Martins, and a black leather biker jacket. As she strode closer, she jingled with enough silver boho jewelry to knock a normal person off kilter.

She whipped off mirrored aviator sunglasses and walked straight at me, ignoring the waiter that tried desperately to seat her. "Viola?" She stuck her hand out and gave mine a firm pump. "Helene Dix. Thanks for getting me out of hell." She hoisted herself on the barstool next to mine and gave Cheryl a nod. "You must be Cheryl."

"Hi, Helene. Nice to meet you."

"Hell?" I asked.

"You know, once upon a time I was out in the field. Getting things done. In people's faces, demanding answers. Now they got me stuck behind a damn desk. Can you believe it? Me? Nice place here." She glanced around approvingly at the steampunk-esque wood and cast iron stools, plank walls, and Edison lightbulbs before flagging down the bartender. "You got anything besides those floofy drinks?"

The bartender gave Helene a look that could only be described as annoyed, his upper lip with its pencil thin mustache curling ever so slightly. The Prohibition was known for its pre-Prohibition cocktails. Not exactly what I would call floofy. "Whatever you want, lady." He waved a tattooed hand to indicate the rows of alcohol on the shelves behind the bar. "Pick your poison."

"Gin and tonic. And throw in a lime wedge."

He nodded. "You got it."

Helene turned to me. "I don't know why they gotta mess around with good alcohol. Straight and simple, that's my motto." She glanced askance at my copper mug sitting neatly on the polished wood bar top. "What the blazes is that?"

"A Michigone Mule."

"Never heard of it."

I took a sip. It was tangy, herbal, and refreshing with just enough kick to make it worthwhile. "I guess it's a take on a Moscow Mule. Vodka, Pimms, lime..."

"Hey, if I wanted a recipe, I'd have called that Giada chick. Now, what is it I can help you with?" She nodded at the bartender as he slid a G & T her way.

Cheryl had told her on the phone exactly what I wanted. In fact, it was Helene herself who'd insisted on driving down here from Portland in person to discuss it. Apparently "getting out of Hell" was top priority even if it meant a nearly two-hour drive. "Krys Marlowe."

"Oh, that piece of work? What's she mixed up in now?" She took a gulp of her G & T and nodded in approval.

"Well, she's dead. And we're trying to figure out who killed her." I might have said it a little louder than intended, but nobody noticed. At two in the afternoon, the place was nearly empty.

Helene eyed me and Cheryl, then gave a bark of laughter. Her face crinkled in amusement. "You're kidding, right? The two of you?"

Cheryl and I exchanged glances. Cheryl shrugged and took a sip of her drink. I turned back to Helene. "Why not us?"

Helene shook her head. "Your funeral, but let me tell you, hun, whoever killed that woman did everyone a favor." The way she said "woman" made it sound like a curse word. She downed the rest of her drink like a sailor and waved the empty glass at the bartender. He gave me a long suffering look before taking the glass from her.

"I understand she was involved in a hit-and-run in Portland. That someone died. I just wasn't clear on the details," I said, watching the bartender refill Helene's drink. "And since you covered the accident, I figured you might have some insight."

"Involved, sort of. Marlowe was the passenger in the car that hit a little boy. Ten years old. Plowed right over the top of him." Helene grabbed her fresh drink and downed it, too. Geez, the woman could outdrink a pirate. "They pretty much had to force her to testify in the trial. When she did, she claimed the driver wasn't at fault. That the kid had run out in the middle of the road without warning."

"Let me guess: the driver got off, "I said, both unsurprised and disgusted.

Helene nodded. "Some suggested that alcohol had been involved. They'd been coming from a club. She lied about that, too. Said they hadn't been drinking."

"Surely the police would have tested the blood alcohol," Cheryl piped up. "I know Bat would have."

"Sure. Of the driver and he was clean as a whistle. But here's the thing." Helene leaned closer. "It's always been my belief that Marlowe was driving. That she's the one that hit the kid. And she was drunk."

"So, they switched places and both lied about it," I said, following her train of thought.

Helene nodded. "The driver got off and nobody ever questioned Krys Marlowe's testimony except the family of that kid." She frowned. "Sad. Really sad."

"Who was the driver?" I asked.

Helene smirked. "It was the daughter. Madison Marlowe."

Chapter 13
Agatha Has A Lead

"Wow. Can you believe that?" I said as a very drunk Helene Dix toddled off to her hotel for the night. I'd been relieved she hadn't planned on driving back to Portland.

Cheryl leaned heavily on the bar, her eyes equally heavy. "It's quite the story."

"Can you believe that Krys Marlowe killed a kid and let her daughter take the blame? No wonder they didn't get along." My mother might be an infuriating busybody, but she would never allow her children to take the blame for something so awful.

"Now, V, don't get your panties in a twist. That was just Helene's take on it. She has no proof."

I snorted. "You met Krys. She wouldn't hesitate to throw an innocent under the bus. Even her own daughter."

Cheryl sighed, running a hand through her spikey hair. "Yeah. Helene is probably right about the whole thing. Krys was not a terribly nice person, but I wouldn't have believed her capable of that."

Which just went to show how nice of a person Cheryl was, because I totally believed Krys Marlowe capable of doing something awful and blaming it on someone else.

"Do you suppose that's why they moved here?" Cheryl asked.

"Probably. I can't imagine the neighbors were friendly

after all that. Probably wanted to move somewhere nobody knew who they were. Start over." The timing was right, too.

"Do you think she knew Dr. Voss was here? In Astoria?"

"Maybe. Likely. Too much of a coincidence for my liking. She probably figured it was a good chance to get a decent job and a little extra money." It seemed like it would be just like Krys, too. Use an old scandal to escape a new one. And profit from it.

"I can't imagine what poor Madison must have felt, being forced to lie. Say she killed someone. Poor kid." Cheryl looked like she might burst into tears any minute.

I wasn't so sure Madison was such a poor, innocent kid. But maybe it explained some things about her behavior. "What about the family?" I said, switching subjects.

Cheryl eyed me. "What do you mean?"

"The family of the kid they killed. They'd have a really good motive for murder if they believed Krys had escaped justice."

Cheryl frowned. "But after all this time?"

"It's only been four years since the death and three since the end of the trial, such as it was. People have committed revenge killings long after that." After all, revenge was a dish best served cold, or so they say.

"True." She agreed. "Maybe we should look into them. See where they are now."

"Good idea." I eyed her. "In the morning. I don't know about you, but I could sleep for a year."

# # #

It was a ringing in my ear that jarred me out of my warm cocoon of sleep. I flailed, trying to free myself of the duvet, until me and half of it were on the floor. With my legs still partially wrapped up, I peered around groggily. My hair was in my face, my eyes dry, and my vision blurry. I ran my tongue over my teeth. My mouth tasted like something died in it. I squinted at the nightstand where something shrilled. My phone.

With a groan, I grabbed it and glared at the screen. Seven thirty. Agatha. Good grief, the woman needed a memo or something. Calling a person before nine in the morning simply wasn't polite.

I considered hitting "ignore" and crawling back into bed. Thing was, if I didn't answer, she'd just keep calling. Turning off the ringer wouldn't work, either, because she'd drive down and pound on my door thinking I was dead or something.

"Hi, Agatha," I said, a little grumpily.

"What's the matter? Sounds like you just woke up."

"Yeah. I did. And that's the matter. Do you know what time it is? I haven't even had my coffee yet."

"Well, you better get a move on. Time's a-wasting." Her voice was entirely too perky.

I rubbed my eyes wearily. "What are you talking about?"

"Didn't I say?"

"No. No, you didn't." I barely refrained from biting

her head off.

"Sorry about that. I've got a lead." She sounded inordinately excited.

"On what?" My brain was still fuzzy from sleep.

"The murder, of course."

I managed to get the duvet unwrapped from my legs and climbed to my feet. "Okay, what's the lead?" I asked as I slogged toward the kitchen in search of coffee.

"Apparently, when Krys Marlowe left Portland three years ago, she didn't just leave because of the hit-and-run."

I blinked. "How'd you know about that?" The only people I'd talked to about the incident were Cheryl and Helene.

"I have my ways." Agatha sounded smug.

I stuck a pod in the coffee maker and shoved a mug below the spout. I hit "start" and went to grab creamer from the fridge. "Fine." My tone was a bit testy, but it was way too early in the morning. "Why else would she have left?" Killing a kid seemed a good enough reason on its own.

"Well three years ago, she was renting an apartment in the city, you see. Really nice place. I spoke to the owner, Maisie Gunn, this morning."

So I wasn't the only one Agatha was bent on torturing. "Uh-huh." Man, I wished she'd speed things up. It was way too early in the morning for these mental gymnastics. I doctored my coffee with creamer and took a long sip. Nirvana. "So what's that got to do with anything?"

"According to Maisie, Krys owed her several months

back rent. Maisie was threatening legal action when Krys skipped out. No forwarding address, nothing. And she lied about her social security number, so Maisie couldn't track her."

"Didn't she do a background search before she let Krys move in?"

Agatha snorted. "Not everyone is as suspicious as you and me."

She had a point. "I still don't see how skipping out on her rent has anything to do with her murder. That was three years ago."

"Well, Maisie needs the money now. Her husband has cancer and she's pretty desperate. She could have driven down here, confronted Krys, demanded her money."

"And then what?" I asked. "Killed her when she refused to pay up?"

"Hey, stranger things have happened. I was watching Aphrodite Jones the other day and some guy got himself murdered over twenty bucks. Can you believe it? This world is going to you-know-where in a handbasket."

I did know where. And it wasn't Disneyland.

"Okay. So Maisie Gunn has motive, albeit a fairly weak motive. Did you tell Bat?" I asked.

"Naw. Thought I'd get your take first. I'll call him next."

I took another sip of coffee. "You do that."

"I really think you should talk to Maisie in person, though. I think it might be imperative to solving the case."

I held back a groan. "I don't want to drive all the way

to Portland."

"Oh, don't worry. She doesn't live in Portland anymore. She lives down near Nehalem Bay. Owns a winery down there."

Well that sounded promising. Nehalem Bay was only a little over an hour away. Plus a winery? "Okay, I'll give it a shot." I found myself agreeing to her scheme.

"Promise?"

"Pinky swear."

And with that, Agatha hung up. I slumped at the table, my chin propped on my hand, eyes still bleary as I sipped my coffee. Lord, save me from the machinations of Agatha.

Chapter 14
Wine Gone Wrong

Lucas returned that evening for an extended stay. It wasn't a surprise, exactly. We'd talked about him coming to Astoria to stay a few weeks and see how he liked living there with the idea that maybe he'd move permanently. I hadn't suggested him moving in with me. Heck, I didn't even let him stay with me during visits. It wasn't for any outdated sense of decorum or whatever. It was just that I'd been single a long time. I liked my personal space. I liked having things just as I wanted them. And I liked having a nice time with Lucas and then having my own personal retreat to return to. Frankly, I wasn't interested in sharing that space full time. Not with Lucas. Not with anyone.

Having someone to spend time with, on the other hand, was nice. With Lucas, it was more than nice. And since he'd been a good sport about previous investigations, I suggested a wine tasting at Maisie Gunn's winery. Two birds with one stone and all that.

Lucas picked me up at four in a turquoise blue 1957 Chevy that belonged to his hotel. How he'd talked them into driving us all the way to Nehalem was beyond me, but then Lucas had his ways. The driver hopped out to open my door. Inside it smelled of old Naugahyde or whatever they used to cover the seats of these old cars. It was cool, though. Very classy and I felt a bit Grace Kelly. I'd even tied a blue-and-pink scarf around my neck and donned my largest pair of sunglasses— even though it would be dark outside in an hour.

"You're looking lovely this evening." Lucas's eyes shone with clear admiration.

"Why, thank you, sir," I said flirtatiously as I removed my sunglasses. Frankly, they'd been a bad idea. I couldn't see a thing. "You're looking quite nice yourself." Understatement of the century. His dark gray suit over a simple white button down shirt set off his tan skin and dark hair. He looked elegant and sophisticated and downright delicious.

The scenery on the way to Nehalem Bay was stunning, to say the least. On the left the forest marched right up to the highway. On the right were vast ocean vistas, the sun slipping toward the sea. It was like a postcard, but I hardly paid attention. I was too busy focused on the man next to me. I still couldn't quite wrap my head around whatever it was we had. This romance thing. It had been unexpected, and I still wasn't entirely sure what to do with it.

The car dropped us off in front of the winery, and Lucas ushered me inside. Soft, classical music floated through the air, and elegantly dressed people hovered about eagerly awaiting the tasting. We stood off by ourselves, content not to mingle for the moment.

The room was wood-paneled and lined with wine bottles. Standing tables made from casks littered the room. The light was slightly dimmed and glowed warmly, making the place feel cozy. It would have been nice if they'd had some chairs.

"How goes the investigation?" Lucas asked, his hand still lightly touching the small of my back. His touch sent shivers up my spine.

"Slowly. I've got more suspects than I know what to do with. And some seriously crazy motives."

"Have the police ruled out the bunco ladies yet?"

"Not entirely," I admitted. "I mean, she died right there in the middle of bunco, but everyone agrees she was a little off and not feeling well from the beginning. The police suspect poison, but haven't said what kind yet. That would determine when she was killed and hopefully clear the bunco ladies." Including yours truly. Though fortunately, Bat hadn't given me any indication I was a real suspect.

"What other suspects have you got?"

I ran through the list, starting with the daughter and how Krys had likely framed her for manslaughter. "Plus, her name is the only one on the life insurance."

"Sounds like excellent motive. Who else?"

I told him about Dr. Voss, Alison Kent, and both Krys's current and ex-husbands. I failed to mention Maisie Gunn. I really didn't consider her much of a suspect and I hadn't had a chance to confront her yet.

Finally, the woman herself appeared and stood in front of the small gathering. "Hello, everyone. Welcome to Gunn Winery. I'm Maisie Gunn."

There was polite clapping and murmurs of approval. I eyed my potential suspect. Maisie was in her late sixties, possibly closer to seventy. Her hair had been dyed medium brown and swept into a smooth chignon at the back of her neck. She wore a simple navy blue shift dress, a string of pearls, and no makeup. Clearly she was going for the simple look. It actually worked for her. She appeared wealthy and sophisticated. Maybe Agatha had been wrong about Maisie's money troubles. Or maybe Maisie was just really good at hiding them.

As black-and-white clad servers wended their way through the crowd handing out small glasses of white wine, Maisie painted a picture of the wine we were sampling first. She tossed around a lot of words like "fruit forward" and "juicy." Several people sniffed the wine, swirled, sniffed some more, took a swig, swished it like mouthwash, and then spit it out in metal buckets placed around the room. I frowned as I sipped mine like a normal person. What a waste of good wine.

"You're going to get drunk if you drink all the samples," Lucas cautioned.

"Good thing I'm not driving, then," I muttered. "You will never catch me spitting out good wine. Losers."

A pair of those losers overheard me and shot a glare over their shoulders. I gave a smug smile back. I had zero tolerance for pretentious twaddle. If you're going to drink wine, then drink the frigging wine, I always say.

By the time we moved on from whites to a nice rosé, I was feeling a little buzzed. Maybe Lucas was right and I should have spit out the wine. With a mental shrug, I sipped the rosé, ignoring the description our hostess was giving. What did I care if it had a pineapple finish? All I cared about was it was delicious.

I really needed to talk to Maisie, but it was impossible

with her in front of everyone, all eyes glued to her as the first red was poured. I didn't even hear the name of the wine or what she said about it. I was too busy thinking about how to approach her, running scenarios through my head.

When the final wine was drunk— or spat— Maisie thanked everyone for coming and turned the whole shindig over to what I assumed was the winery manager. He was a fairly young man in his mid-to-late thirties with sandy hair and a slender figure. He looked enough like Maisie I was betting he was her son, even though she'd only introduced him as "John." He began encouraging people to take home their favorite wines. Soon everyone was fawning over various bottles and asking about case pricing.

"Come on." I grabbed Lucas's hand and dragged him toward the door where Maisie had disappeared. He resisted. I turned to face him. "What's the matter?"

"That door is marked 'employees only.'"

I frowned. Like that had ever stopped him. "So?"

He eyed me carefully, face expressionless. "So why do you want to go in there?"

"Because I need to talk to Maisie Gunn."

He pulled his hand out of mine, his posture suddenly stiff. "And why is that, I wonder?" Was it just me or was he starting to sound a little angry?

"She knew Krys Marlowe back in the day. She might know something about the murder."

"Seriously? You dragged me here just so you could confront some poor, innocent lady?"

I stared at him. What was his problem? "We don't know she's innocent. She might be a murderer."

"So you thought you'd pretend to go on a date with me just so you could... what? Stake her out? Interrogate her? You do realize you're not the police, right?"

The lightbulb went on. So that was his problem. He was pissed I was using our date to investigate a witness. Which was kind of silly. "Don't be ridiculous..."

"Ridiculous?" It came out a bit loud, and I winced as half the gathering turned around to stare at us. "Excuse me if I thought for a moment you'd put me ahead of your little investigation."

"Lucas..."

"Next time you want to investigate, leave me out of it." He stomped off toward the bar and the rest of the gathering, his entire body bristling with angry energy.

I stared after him baffled. Geez, men could be so temperamental. But I had a job to do. This crime wasn't going to solve itself.

I pushed my way through the "employees only" door and found myself in a small office barely big enough to hold a desk and a computer. Maisie Gunn glanced up from the computer, startled. "Can I help you?"

"I hope so," I said, holding out my hand. "I'm Viola Roberts."

Maisie shook my hand tentatively. "The author?"

I was surprised she'd heard of me. I did all right, but it wasn't like I was famous or anything. "Yes, actually."

"Ah. My sister enjoys your novels. She'll be jealous I met you." She smiled at me as she took off her reading glasses. "How can I help?"

"Are you familiar with a woman named Krys Marlowe?"

Her expression tightened. "Unfortunately, yes."

"Did you know she was murdered a few days ago?"

Genuine surprise crossed her face, but she didn't appear upset or sad. "I hadn't heard. How terrible for her family. What happened?"

"Poison, most likely."

"Suspects?" she asked. She hadn't even blinked at the mention of poison.

"A lot of them. None of them popping at the moment."

She nodded. "Not a surprise. Did you meet her?"

"Yes."

"Then you understand."

I did. "She was an interesting woman."

"She was a pain in the butt, you mean. Horrible person. She probably had more enemies than there are people in this town. Everywhere she went, she had a habit of stirring up trouble."

"So I've heard. I understand she rented a property from you?"

A muscle flexed in her jaw. "A few years ago back in Portland, I rented a unit to her and her daughter. At first things were fine, but then after a few months she stopped paying rent. I threatened to evict her and she skipped town."

"How much did she owe you?" I asked, knowing it was a nosey question.

"Nearly six months. I felt sorry for her. Never again." She glanced up and gave me a hard look. "But I didn't kill her."

"Even though she put you in a touchy financial position right at the time your husband was ill and dying?"

She seemed surprised. "How did you know that?"

"I have my ways." My phrase echoed Agatha's.

Maisie sighed. "It's true. It was a bad time. But that was a year ago. My husband has passed, and I've moved on."

"And the money?"

"My husband had a good life insurance policy. In the end I didn't need the money. And now I have my dream."

I glanced around. "The winery?"

She gave me a genuinely happy smile. "Proof positive that it's never too late to start over and live your dreams."

She seemed like a genuinely nice lady, but I had to know. "I suppose you have an alibi for the murder?"

"When was it again?"

I gave her the date and time.

She slid her glasses on and peered at a calendar app on the computer screen. "I was right here at the winery. Where I usually am. The boys are in and out. I'm sure they can confirm if the police need it." She gave me a pointed look.

"One last question," I said, ignoring the look. "What did you think about Krys's daughter, Madison?"

Maisie leaned back in her chair thoughtfully. "She was an interesting child. Quiet. Shy. And totally railroaded by an overbearing mother. She had potential. I think with another sort of parent, she really could have shone."

I thanked her and hurried back to the wine room. I was tempted to cross Maisie off the list, but her alibi was a bit shaky in my opinion. For now, she was staying.

I caught Lucas's scowl from across the room. Oh, boy. This didn't bode well. I was going to have some serious explaining to do.

He jerked his head toward the door, and I sighed heavily, the wine buzz quickly evaporating. I guess we were leaving.

Chapter 15
Playing Detective

The next day I woke with a pounding headache. I downed two full glasses of water plus a couple of Tylenol before moving on to coffee. I wanted to shout at the workmen hammering so early in the morning until I realized it was my own throbbing head.

I sat hunched over the table for I-don't-know-how-long before I managed to stagger to the shower. Warm water and rose-scented shower gel helped immensely. As did another cup of coffee and another couple of Tylenol. I managed to get down a slice of dry toast, but that was it. My stomach revolted over the thought of anything else. I made a mental note to never attend a wine tasting again. I just didn't have the self control.

My phone pinged. It was Lucas. I frowned as I read the curt message. He was on his way back to Portland. No mention of talking to me later or coming down for another visit. He must be truly pissed off. Which was ridiculous. What did he expect me to do? Ignore the fact that a prime suspect was right in front of my face? Granted I'd set the whole thing up and claimed it was a "date" so I could sort of see his point, but come on. At least I'd spent time with him.

I tried to ignore the stab of guilt. I was only marginally successful. Probably I'd have to grovel later, but right now I just couldn't deal. My head hurt, my stomach was on the lurch, and I still had a murder to solve. Oh, yeah...

and there was that looming book deadline to boot.

I called Cheryl. "Hey," I said when she answered. "How do you feel about a trip down south?"

"How far down south?" she asked with more suspicion than was warranted.

"Lincoln City."

There was a pause. "You're going to question Malcom's girlfriend, aren't you?"

"Not question. We've got a viewing. She's a real estate agent, remember? And if I just happen to mention I know her boyfriend, well…"

"You're so devious," she giggled. "Give me an hour."

"You got it." I'd need an hour to pull myself together. Heck, I wasn't even sure that was enough.

I downed another glass of water, then parked myself at my vanity to make myself presentable. I doubted Diana Landford would be impressed if I showed up looking like death warmed over. It was going to take a lot of concealer to hide the dark circles under my eyes.

Exactly an hour later, I pulled up in front of Cheryl's condo and texted to let her know I was there. A few minutes later, she was climbing into the car looking smart in a pair of black slacks, a royal blue top and a tailored charcoal jacket. In her hand she clutched a red purse as big as she was.

"Look at you, all dressed up."

"You said we needed to impress this woman." She eyeballed my own dark jeans and mulberry tunic. Not exactly the height of fashion, but comfortable and reasonably stylish.

"So I did. She'll think you're the fashionable friend."

"I am the fashionable friend," she said smugly.

Alas, it was true. Less because I didn't know fashion and more because fashion for the curvy woman was somewhat limited. Plus, I'd rather be comfortable than stylish any day of the week—which was why my wardrobe consisted mostly of pajamas.

Lincoln City was a two-and-a-half-hour drive away at top speed with no traffic. The day was sunny despite the chill in the air, and the ocean glittered like diamonds along the right side of Highway 101. It was the perfect day for a drive. Since it was mid-week, traffic was fairly light and we made good time, arriving an hour before our meeting with Diana Landford.

I pulled into the local Pig 'n Pancake—one of those coastal chain diners overly fond of Formica—where we made quick work of eggs benedict and more coffee while we discussed our strategy for handling Diana. The coffee was sub-par, so I dumped in four packets of sugar and an equal amount of cream.

"I think we should be blunt," I said wincing at the bitter taste of the cheap coffee. "Just go straight at her. Accuse her of murdering Krys."

"You think she'll fall for that?" Cheryl scoffed. "This woman is a salesperson. She's used to bluffing."

"True. If not outright lying."

"Not all salespeople are liars," Cheryl insisted. "But she's likely used to working with difficult people. Getting up in her face probably won't get us far."

"Okay, fine. We'll be subtle then. Mention we know

Malcom. Tell her he referred us to her."

"Sympathize with his loss, which is therefore her loss." Cheryl was getting into the game now.

I frowned. "You think she'll actually care that Krys is dead? I would imagine she'd be celebrating."

Cheryl thought it over. "Maybe. So what? Play it by ear?"

"I think that's best. If she acts like she's happy, we talk about what a horrible person Krys was. It won't be a lie."

"Viola!" Cheryl said in a shocked tone.

"What? It won't. She was terrible and you know it."

"Fine. Fine. And if she acts sad?"

"We sympathize. All sweetness and whatnot. Poor Mal. Must be so hard on him. Either way, hopefully we'll get something out of her. At least find out if she has an alibi." I tossed a few bills on the table and stood up.

Cheryl groaned as we walked toward the exit of the Pig 'n Pancake. "I swear, I don't know how you come up with these schemes."

"Natural brilliance, of course."

She snorted. "If you say so."

We didn't have far to go to find the house we were supposedly viewing. It was a nice place. Pretty standard beach fair with weathered shingles and a pebbled front yard. The picket fence needed paint, but there was a decent view of the ocean, if partially blocked by the houses in front of it. The door stood open, and the scent of cookies baking wafted out.

"That's a trick of the trade," Cheryl said softly. "I saw it on one of those house makeover shows. Makes people think of home so they're more likely to buy."

"Too bad it's wasted on us." Diana would be sorely disappointed if she thought chocolate chip cookies would sway us into buying a house in Lincoln City. I would not, however, refuse them if offered. I'm not an idiot.

As we stepped across the threshold, a thirty-something woman with bright red hair wearing a navy blue power suit stepped out from what I assumed was the kitchen. Her nude pumps made a clacking sound on the hardwood floor. "Ladies." She held out her hands expansively as if welcoming us into her space. "I'm Diana Landford. Welcome. I'm so excited to show you this home. I think it's just what you're looking for."

"Oh, really?" I asked. "What a relief. Seems like we've been looking forever." I glanced around. The place was entirely uninteresting with uninspired blank white walls, wood floors that were too pale to be stylish, and zero furniture. "It seems pretty perfect so far. Malcom did say you were a genius when it came to finding houses."

She simpered a bit. "Well, Malcom would know."

"Did you help him find his house? It's so lovely."

"Well, no," she admitted. "But he's a very smart man."

"Of course. So sad about his wife, though. Poor man." Diana stiffened a bit. "Yes. Very sad."

"Did you know Krys?" Cheryl asked vaguely as she wandered into the kitchen as if not particularly interested in the answer. I gave her mega points for acting.

Diana gave a little cough into her hand. "I never met her." Which wasn't entirely an answer. She wasn't acting happy about Krys Marlowe's death, but she wasn't acting sad, either. More like uncomfortable.

I leaned a little closer. "I was there, you know."

Diana's eyes widened. "When she died?" Was it me, or was her voice a little strangled?

I nodded. "I found the body."

She touched her lips with her perfectly manicured fingertips, a little gasp escaping. "How horrible."

"Mm-hmm. The police interrogated me for hours." Total exaggeration. Bat had questioned me for all of fifteen minutes. "Did they question you?"

She appeared startled, fingers straying to toy with her chunky gold necklace. "Why would they do that?"

"Well, you knew her right? Or rather her husband. I think they're questioning everyone the Marlowes know. Just to be safe, you know. Cover all their bases. I imagine they'll want your alibi. You have one, right?"

She licked her lips. "Oh, I'm sure I do. I was probably working." She didn't sound sure. "Don't you want to see the house?"

"Oh, yeah, lead on."

We followed her as she clacked her way through the living and dining rooms, pointing out what I'm sure she thought were interesting benefits of the house. She sounded a little rattled. Good. Time to push.

"Where were you, by the way?" I asked.

She stumbled to a stop. "Excuse me?"

"The night Krys died. You weren't in Astoria were you? That could look bad."

"Really bad," Cheryl agreed.

Diana licked her lips. "Um, no. No, I wasn't."

"Well, that's a relief," I said. "If the police can check your alibi, then you should be good. You have one right?"

"I was...I was with my boyfriend." Diana lifted her chin. "At a hotel."

"Which hotel?" Cheryl asked.

"I don't know. It had a fir tree on it. Why do you care?" Diana was clearly flustered. "I'm sure they can check if they ask."

"Oh, good," I said, feigning relief. "You seem like a nice person, and I hate for them to suspect you. Trust me—it's not fun."

Whether from embarrassment or anger it was hard to tell, but Diana's cheeks were scarlet. However, she was clearly determined to carry on the viewing. "Shall we continue?"

"You know," I said, pausing to look around. "I really don't think I'm feeling this place. Are you?" I turned to Cheryl.

"No. It's a little bijou."

I nodded. "Very bijou. Thanks for your time."

And with that we strode quickly from the house and took off in a squeal of tires.

Cheryl started laughing the minute we hit the highway. I stared at her. "What's so funny?"

"I thought she was going to pass out. Or hit you in the face."

I glared at her. "You make it sound like either would have been acceptable."

"Well, it certainly would have been interesting."

I gritted my teeth. "In any case, she's got an alibi. And,

unfortunately, she also gives Malcom an alibi." It was so frustrating. Just when I thought I had it figured out.

"So they both have motives, but they also have alibis. So it couldn't have been them."

"I guess not." I tightened my grip on the steering wheel. "What I need to do is talk to the daughter. I have a feeling she's hiding something."

# # #

When we got back to Astoria, I dropped Cheryl off at her condo before deciding to hit Bakeology for dinner. I still had a bit of a headache, and the trip had worn me out. Cooking simply wasn't on the agenda.

It was misting lightly as I ducked inside the warm bakery and ordered a chicken-and-mushroom pot pie. I'd just sat down to eat when Madison barreled through the doorway. She hesitated when she saw me, but I waved her over.

"I'll buy you dinner." I figured a bribe wouldn't hurt.

"Whatever." She stomped to the table and sat down across from me. She was wearing all black as usual, and had big black smudges of eyeliner under her eyes. I wasn't sure if it was deliberate or if she'd fallen asleep and smudged her makeup. Either way, she looked like a raccoon.

I ordered Madison a pot pie and some coffee and we sat for a moment in awkward silence, munching on our food. Finally I decided to dive in. Now or never.

"Listen, Madison, I don't want to keep nagging you

about this, but this is important. Your mother was murdered, and you have a very good motive."

She gave me a sullen look and returned to picking at her dark red nail polish. "No, I don't."

"Yeah, actually, you do. Money. Hello?"

She frowned. "What are you talking about?"

"You told me about the insurance when I was at your house."

"Ain't my house."

Somehow I managed to bite back the snarky reply. "Malcom's house. In any case, you get a hefty sum from your mother's life insurance. Don't you remember telling me about it?"

Madison ground her teeth. "Like I care about the stupid money."

"Well, the police will care," I pointed out. "The unemployed daughter who argues with her mother comes into a big chunk of change at mother's death. Sounds pretty suspicious to me."

Madison snorted. "That's where you're wrong."

"Really? Do tell."

She sighed heavily as if I was the most stupid person on the planet. "Look, lady, not that it's any of your business, but my dad—my real dad—has plenty of money. He gives me an allowance every month. And if I run out, he's happy to give me more."

That was news to me. "Really? I thought the police were after Jerry for identity theft."

She breathed another long, suffering sigh. "Jerry isn't my father. He married Mom when I was two."

"Oh." That was news to me.

"My real father left when I was a baby. Not that I blame him. My mother...you met her. Anyway, he's got this new family. Wife, kids, dog... the whole thing. He'd rather pretend I didn't exist. So as long as I don't come around, he makes sure I've got more than enough. Dude, there's like over twenty thousand in my savings account right now." She rolled her eyes like I was an idiot.

"But surely the life insurance is substantial," I pointed out.

"It's only a quarter of a million." She said it like I might say it was twenty dollars.

"I don't know about you," I said, "but where I come from that's a lot of money."

Madison shrugged. "That's chump change compared to what my dad will give me if I want it."

"Why don't you?" I asked. "Take it, I mean."

"Because I'm not greedy," Madison snapped. "I don't need millions. I have enough that I can do what I want. Chill. Do art. Work for charity. Whatever. And I'm happy to take it because he owes me. But more than that is a waste."

It was a weird way of looking at things. Not a lot of people would have felt that way, but it made a certain kind of sense.

"Basically, I don't need the insurance money. I mean, yay, great, whatever. But I don't care."

So there went Madison's motive. Sure, she'd probably find a use for the money, but she hadn't needed it. If she wanted a big chunk, she could have gone after her rich dad. Once again, I was running out of suspects.

"Still, the police are going to want to know if you have an alibi." I knew she did, of course, but I wanted to hear it from her mouth.

She snorted. "I do."

"And?"

"I was with the mayor's son."

Which was about as good an alibi as it got.

Shéa MacLeod

Chapter 16
Hemlock and Bunco

"Ruby is dead."

I pulled the phone away from my ear and stared at the screen a minute before replacing it. "Say that again."

"Ruby Rogers. She's dead." Agatha's voice broke into a sob.

"Ruby? From bunco?" I couldn't quite wrap my head around it.

"Yes. Can you believe it?"

"What happened?" It was all I could manage to get out.

"Her niece found her this morning dead as a doornail. The police think it was hemlock poisoning." Another sob escaped her.

"Hemlock?" I felt like an idiot repeating everything, but it was all I could get out.

"That's what killed Krys Marlowe."

I frowned. "How do you know?" Though why I bothered to ask, I don't know. Agatha was a font of information, usually very accurate. "Never mind," I interrupted before she could launch into a lengthy explanation. "Why do they think Ruby was killed with the same poison?"

"Because she had the same symptoms right before she died."

Well, that wasn't good. "But why Ruby?"

"I don't know," Agatha wailed. "But whoever the

murderer is, they're bumping off the bunco group!"

A slight exaggeration since Krys hadn't technically been part of the group, but a sub. I still couldn't wrap my head around Ruby's death, though. Why? She was such a nice woman. Kind-hearted and generous. Why would anyone want to kill her? And what did it have to do with Krys Marlowe? The deaths had to be connected. I couldn't see any other option. It would be too big of a coincidence for two women from bunco to die within days of each other of the same poison. Even Bat would have to admit to that.

My phone beeped letting me know there was another incoming call. A quick glance at the caller ID told me our esteemed detective was on the other line. "Agatha, I gotta go."

"But—"

"I'll talk to you later." I hung up before she could get another word out and answered Bat's call. "Detective. To what do I owe this pleasure?" Pretty sure he heard the sarcasm.

"I need you to come down to the station, Viola."

"Let me guess, you think someone in the bunco group killed both Krys and Ruby and you want to grill me about it."

He let out a frustrated groan. "Agatha?"

"Got it in one."

"Who needs social media with that one on the loose?" I was pretty sure the question was rhetorical so I didn't reply. "Will you come down?"

"I can be there in fifteen. As long as you bring the

donuts."

"Not all cops eat donuts." Was it me, or was he grinding his teeth?

"The point remains, I want donuts. They will make me very cooperative."

"Fine," he snarled.

"Chocolate cake donuts."

Bat hung up.

# # #

"I don't know what to tell you," I said, crossing my arms over my chest and one leg over the other. I would have rather been anywhere but the police station. Like out there solving the murders, for instance. "I have no idea who poisoned Krys and I definitely don't know who poisoned Ruby. Also, there are no donuts. I was very specific about the donuts." Maybe if I focused on the lack of donuts, I wouldn't start bawling like a baby over Ruby.

Bat ignored me. He'd shoved me into a tiny closet-sized space barely big enough for a table and two chairs. It was claustrophobic to say the least. The place stank of cheap aftershave and stale coffee and the walls were painted a depressing shade of greenish gray.

"I know it's ridiculous," he said, "but I need your alibi."

"Fine. When was Ruby poisoned?"

"The medical examiner says anytime between three and five hours before her death."

I tapped my foot in exasperation. "Which was?"

"Midnight. Give or take an hour. Her niece found her at nine this morning. They were supposed to have breakfast together."

"Poor girl. That must have been such a shock." I'd never met Ruby's niece, but I knew they were close. Ruby had talked about her all the time.

"They had to give her a sedative," Bat said grimly. "Now. Your alibi?"

I mulled it over. "So, between 7 PM and 9 PM last night? Cheryl and I got back from Lincoln City about five..."

His eyes narrowed. "What were you doing in Lincoln City?"

"Oh, you know. Lovely day for a drive."

"Viola." There was a dangerous edge to his voice and the muscles in his jaw flexed dangerously.

"Fine. If you must know we were there to talk to Diana whatsername. Landford. Malcom Marlowe's mistress. She wasn't terribly upset about Krys's death, and you know she has an excellent motive."

He pinched the bridge of his nose between his thumb and forefinger. "You got back to Astoria around five..."

"Oh, right. I dropped Cheryl off at home—she's on deadline—and then I grabbed a quick bite at Bakeology. Sandy makes the best pot pies, you know. The chicken and mushroom is ridiculous. And have you tried their curry pasties?"

"After dinner. What did you do after dinner," he bit out.

"I talked to Madison. That's Krys Marlowe's

daughter."

"Yes. I know."

"Well, I had a chat with her about the money she got from her mom's death. I mean it gave her a great motive except apparently her dad is filthy rich."

"Yes. I know." He was repeating himself. I might drive the man to drink yet.

"So, I was done with that by maybe six thirty. So I headed to The Prohibition and had a couple of drinks. Chatted with the bartender. I was home around ten. Wrote for an hour or so, watched Bill Maher, and was in bed by twelve thirty."

"Your alibi is The Prohibition."

"Yep." I grinned. "Good one, huh?"

"And how about the day of the bunco game? Where were you?"

"Was Krys poisoned the same time before the game? Three to five hours?"

He gritted his teeth. "The medical examiner says it was earlier. Maybe as much as eight hours."

"Huh. Okay. So bunco starts at seven. She was dead by eight. So as early as noon."

"Your math skills are stellar."

I ignored his sarcasm. "I was with my mother."

"Your mother?" he repeated.

"That's what I said," I said smugly. "See, Mom came to town for the day and left just before bunco."

A line appeared between his eyes as he processed that information. "Did you go anywhere? See anyone?"

"You could say that," I said dryly. "We had coffee and

breakfast at Caffeinate. Swung by Lucy's bookshop. At some point we hit the Tiki bar. Then we toured just about every shop in town."

"So if I ask around, people will remember you?"

"I would imagine so. My mother is very… memorable."

He rubbed his forehead as if suddenly developing a headache. "What time did you get to Agatha's that night for bunco?"

"Six forty-five on the dot. I pretty much always get there fifteen minutes before. Cheryl answered the door. She can confirm."

"Fine. Okay." He slid me a sideways look. "How is Cheryl handling this?"

I paused for a beat. "Why don't you ask her yourself?"

He grimaced. "I don't imagine her new boyfriend would appreciate it."

I snorted. "Duke? That loser? Please. You know as well as I do that he took off back to Portland ages ago. She hasn't heard from him since." I leaned forward. "Listen, if you don't make your move at some point in the not-too-distant future, you're going to end up an unremarkable footnote in Cheryl's life. Is that really what you want?"

He cleared his throat. "It wouldn't be appropriate to get involved personally with a suspect."

I stared at him then burst out laughing. "You really consider Cheryl a suspect?"

"I consider everyone a suspect." He didn't even crack a smile.

I figured I'd better switch the subject before I bashed him upside the head with my empty coffee cup. Plus, there were still some things I didn't know. "Do you know how the poison was administered?" I asked.

He narrowed his eyes. "This is an ongoing investigation."

"Don't give me that. Come on," I wheedled. "I might be able to give you some information or something."

"Fine. It looks like Krys was probably dosed with the green smoothie she has every day for lunch."

I wrinkled my nose. "Serves her right. No one should drink those things. But how could someone spike it?"

"Apparently she would make a batch in the morning and drink it throughout the day, only eating a proper dinner." He tried to remain impassive, but I could see his nose wrinkling. He clearly thought smoothie drinking in place of real food was as crazy as I did.

"Ah, one of those people. So someone could have snuck into her house and dumped hemlock into the refrigerated smoothie. She'd have never noticed. Those things already taste nasty."

"Exactly." He sounded tired.

"And Ruby?"

"Her salad at dinner. There was some in the garbage. We found traces of hemlock leaves and root mixed in."

"Wow. Somebody really wanted those women dead." So much so they'd been willing to accidentally poison anyone who drank or ate the poisoned food. Not that anyone in their right minds would drink a green smoothie. Or eat salad.

"And unfortunately we still don't know who it was. At this moment the entire bunco group could be at risk." He gave me a hard look. "Including you."

Chapter 17
The Problem With Blackmail

My bet for prime suspect was still Dr. Voss. I didn't care what he said; I was sure Krys Marlowe had been blackmailing him. Why he needed to murder Ruby was beyond me. Maybe Ruby knew something? Had seen something? Could Krys have let a secret slip? Something Voss didn't want the world to know?

After leaving the police station, I swung by the doctor's office and parked next to his fancy Mercedes. With a grim expression plastered on my face, I marched in. Alison barely looked up from buffing her nails as I marched past her desk and into Voss's office. Apparently I was now a regular.

"What are you doing here?" Dr. Voss glared at me from his place by the bookshelf. He'd been flipping through a medical text. There were crumbs on the front of his lab coat. Evidently someone had gotten him donuts. Which made me annoyed at Bat all over again.

"I want to know why you killed Ruby."

He blanched. "Wh-what?"

"Ruby Rogers is dead. Murdered last night by the same person who killed Krys Marlowe."

Voss sat heavily in his chair which gave an ominous squeak at the increase in weight. "That's not possible. Mrs. Marx can't be dead."

"I know Krys was blackmailing you," I said, barging ahead. "You killed her, didn't you? And then you killed poor Ruby because she found out what you did. Was she trying to blackmail you, too?" Not that I believed that of Ruby. Not for a second.

"No. No. You've got this all wrong." Voss was looking sweaty and pale.

I sat down across from him. "Then explain it to me. Carefully. Because my next stop is the police station."

He rubbed his forehead. "Krys was blackmailing me, yes. But it was so stupid."

"What was she blackmailing you over?"

"I had an affair with a patient," he admitted.

My eyes widened. "Oh, my, doctor. That isn't good. You could lose your license."

"Not exactly. You see, she was no longer my patient once we started the affair. So legally I'm free and clear."

The lightbulb went on. "But this is a small town. Your reputation might not have recovered. And then there's your wife..."

"Yes," he said. "You understand my situation. Paying her was easier. She wasn't asking that much. A few hundred dollars a month. I could have afforded more, to be honest. But it worked for both of us. She got a tax-free boost to her income. I put it under "miscellaneous expenses" and took a tax write-off. It all worked out. I had no reason to kill her."

"She didn't demand more money?"

"No. Not at all. At first, I thought she would, but apparently she preferred to have large numbers of victims at lower monthly costs to ensure they kept paying. It was quite smart actually." He sounded as if he almost admired her for it.

It made sense. If Krys was willing to blackmail both Alison Kent and the doctor, no doubt there were others in town she'd been blackmailing for money or favors. Added up, it was probably a nice supplemental income. And nobody got too stubborn about paying since she kept it within their means. Smart indeed.

"Do you know who else she was blackmailing?"

"I'm afraid not," he said.

"Then how do you know there were others?" I asked.

"Krys told me," he admitted. "She just wouldn't tell me who. She was very proud of her little side business."

"You've heard about Ruby Rogers?" I watched him carefully, but he didn't flinch. He just seemed sad.

"Unfortunately. Poor woman. But if Ruby was murdered because she knew something about all this, it had nothing to do with me," the doctor continued. "I would never hurt her. She was an old family friend. My mother went to school with her, for goodness' sake. I dated her daughter before I married my wife."

"People have murdered family friends before," I pointed out.

"But I had no reason. Ruby didn't know anything about the agreement between Krys and myself. No one did."

That he knew of, anyway. And I guess that was the point. If he didn't know, then he had no motive to kill anyone over it.

"I'm still taking this to Bat. Unless you have an alibi."

He winced. "I don't…"

I just gave him a look.

He shifted uncomfortably. "Fine. I was with a, er, friend of mine."

The way he said it, I assumed it was a lover. Cheating on his wife. How unoriginal. "Name?"

A muscled flexed in his jaw. "Orlando."

"So you were having a gay affair."

His eyes widened and he barked a laugh. "Not at all. Not that there's anything wrong with that," he said hastily. "I just prefer women, you understand."

"So who is this Orlando then?"

"You could call him my gambling buddy. We frequently meet at the casino down the coast for a bit of gambling. The night Krys died, that was where I was."

"And last night? Where were you?" I asked.

"The same."

I frowned. "I don't understand why you didn't just admit this before. What's the big deal?"

"I prefer my wife doesn't find out about my... activities. She doesn't like the gambling. She gets... agitated. The last time she caught me, she made me swear not to go again. That if I gambled again she'd leave me. So you see, I didn't want it becoming public knowledge." He gave me an apologetic smile.

It was my turn to grind my teeth. Honestly. If he'd just admitted to the gambling, all of this could have been gotten out of the way ages ago. "And you haven't told Bat?"

"He's never asked. Apparently, I'm not on his radar. Only yours." He gave me a pointed look that spoke volumes about his opinion on my nosiness. He cleared his throat. "Although he does know about the break-in."

"What break-in?"

"My office was broken into shortly after Krys died. I don't suppose you had anything to do with that?" He glared at me.

"Why would I break into your office?" I asked, genuinely confused.

"Your little investigation. Trying to dig up evidence."

I laughed. "Doctor, you watch too much television. No, I did not break into your office." I hadn't needed to. It was easy enough to stroll through the front door. A thought struck me. "What did they take?"

"That's what's strange. As far as I can tell, they didn't take a thing."

"That's weird."

"You're telling me." Voss was clearly not happy about it. "There is a lot of sensitive information in my files."

That gave me an idea. "What about your files? Were they disturbed in any way? Like maybe somebody looked at them?"

"I'm afraid that's not something I can share," he said stiffly.

Fine. I had other ways of finding out. "Okay. Well, thanks for your time."

"I trust you will stop harassing me over this little matter?"

"If by 'little matter,' you are referring to people being murdered horribly, then yes. I'm convinced you didn't do it," I assured him.

"That's a relief," he said dryly.

Out in the lobby, Alison was still messing around with her nails. She'd moved from buffing to painting and the stench of nail polish flooded the small space. Half her nails were already hooker red.

"Hey, Alison," I said, leaning a hip against her desk. "Nice day, huh?" Outside the rain had started coming down in earnest. It pattered the windows, turning the outside world into a blurry watercolor.

"What do you want?" Her tone was sulky, but I ignored it.

"Voss says the place was broken into a few nights ago."

This time she looked up, suddenly excited about a little gossip. "Yeah. It was crazy. I got here and the door was open. Like not wide open, but a little bit. And the lock was busted."

"Wow. Scary. What did you do?"

"Called the cops, of course." She swiped red on another nail. "Whoever did it was long gone, and they didn't take anything, so the police took my statement and left." She shrugged as if it happened every other day.

"Did you look at the files? Maybe they took something from there?" I asked.

"Nope. The files were fine. I mean, obviously someone had gone through them and one of the files was sticking up, but nothing taken."

So somebody wanted information on a particular patient. "Whose file was it?"

"I'm not sure I should tell you. There are rules, you

know. Dr. Voss might get mad if I tell you."

"Hey, I'm a patient here, too, you know. I have a right to know what's happening with my information." Not that I'd used Voss since I'd transferred my files here, but that was beside the point.

"It wasn't yours," Alison admitted. "It was right next to yours."

"Whose was it?"

"Ruby Rogers," she admitted.

That surprised me. "What would they want with Ruby's file?"

"No idea. She's just some old lady that comes in whenever her arthritis flares up. There's nothing interesting about her except that bee allergy. Well, and the fact she died last night. Poor thing."

Bee allergy. That was weird. Good thing she wasn't the one who found a bee in her kitchen. She could have ended up dead even sooner.

Shéa MacLeod

Chapter 18
Bat Is A Bully

"I don't know what you think you're doing." Bat was storming back and forth on the sidewalk in front of my house, completely ignoring the rain that pelted down soaking him from head to toe. I'd been nearly home when he'd started following me in his unmarked police car. He'd tried to pull me over, but since I was a block away from the house, I'd just driven home and parked in my driveway like a normal person.

"I don't know what you're talking about." Actually I had a pretty good idea, but I figured it was best to ignore such things. If you don't admit what you've done, they can't hang you for it. Or something like that.

"I got a call from Dr. Voss. He's complaining about you pestering him and his people. You're poking your nose where it doesn't belong, aren't you?" Bat loomed over me like an avenging angel.

"Not true," I said haughtily, straightening to my full five-foot-five. Admittedly, it wasn't very impressive when compared to Bat's six-foot frame. "This is very much my business. It involves my friends, and since you seem to think one of them did it, I'm going to prove you wrong."

He pinched the bridge of his nose between his thumb and forefinger. A sure sign he was at the end of his patience. "Viola—"

"Don't you 'Viola' me," I snapped. "I have every right to look into this."

"No. No, you don't. This is a police matter, and if you don't butt out—"

"What? What are you going to do?" I crossed my arms and glared at him, ignoring the fact that the damp was quickly turning my hair into a frizzy mess.

"I'm going to arrest you for obstruction."

I snorted. "Please. I'll be out in five minutes, and you know it."

"Stay out of this. It's not your business. And it's not safe." He poked his nose dangerously close to my face. If he wasn't careful, he was going to lose an appendage. "This person is killing people. Don't you get that?"

"Duh," I snapped. "I'm not an idiot."

"Could have fooled me," he snarled.

That did it. "You. Get off my lawn." And with that I turned and stormed into my house, slamming the door behind me.

I paused for a moment to fume. I swear if I'd been a cartoon, there'd have been steam pouring out of my ears. Instead, I followed the only avenue left to me. I grabbed a towel for my hair, then stomped into my office, flipped open my laptop, and started writing while simultaneously muttering to myself.

"The sleazy sheriff of Butler's Gulch..." No, wait. That wasn't fair. Bat wasn't sleazy. I hit the backspace key. "The sheriff of Butler's Gulch was a mean and unreasonable man." Yes. That was it. Very accurate. "He strode around like he owned the town, was rude to old ladies, and thought he was better than everyone. Until the day Jake Sutter rode into town and shot him dead." Yes, indeed. I was feeling better already. I pounded on the keys for the next hour or so, gleefully murdering Bat several times over. My readers were going to love it.

Shéa MacLeod

Chapter 19
Mostly Dead

Cheryl interrupted my Bat-murdering-spree with a text asking if I wanted to meet at The Prohibition for cocktails. Did I ever. Although killing Bat in creative ways had certainly taken the edge off of my outrage, I could definitely use a stiff drink. Especially considering I hadn't heard from Lucas since he went back to Portland in a tizzy. I should probably call him, but I was avoiding the issue. My middle name is "Procrastination." At least that's what my mother always said.

I wiggled into a pair of skinny jeans, knee-high boots, and a red tank top with a long, black cardigan over it. The boots made me feel badass. The cardigan hit my knees almost like a cape. It was like being a superhero. Maybe I needed a cool name? I laughed at my lunacy as I pushed through the door to The Prohibition.

Old timey music floated out from the stereo. The chipper tune, plucked out on banjos, made me tap my feet. Cheryl waved to me from across the dim bar. She'd gotten a booth next to the window. I joined her, sliding onto the banquet across from her.

"You're all dressed up tonight," Cheryl said, giving me the once over. "Special occasion?" She wore simple blue jeans, Chuck Taylor sneakers in red, and a gray hoodie over a Wonder Woman t-shirt.

"No occasion. I just felt... sassy."

"You always feel sassy." She grinned.

"More sassy than usual."

She laughed. "I ordered drinks already. Got you a mule."

"Perfect." Helene Dix might not have been impressed, but I loved The Prohibition's mules.

I hadn't been sitting a full minute when a server brought over our drinks. The mule hit the spot, and I drank it quickly as Cheryl and I chatted about our latest works. She was currently making her first foray into the romance market with a romantic suspense novel. Usually she wrote thrillers, so it wasn't too much of a departure. I told her about creating the sheriff character for my latest western romance.

"I can't believe you killed off Bat's character," she said with a giggle. "That's hilarious."

"Better than killing Bat," I said. I raised my hand to motion to the waiter to bring another round. "That would probably get me arrested."

"Probably," Cheryl said dryly as the waiter dropped off new drinks and collected our empties.

I took a swallow of my mule and made a face. "Ew."

"What's wrong?" Cheryl asked over the rim of her martini glass.

"It tastes funny." I took another sip to be sure. I was right the first time. It definitely tasted off.

"Well, get a new one then." She waved at the bartender who rolled her eyes, but sent the waiter back.

"Something wrong, ladies?" he asked earnestly, blond curls shining under the warm glow of the lights above the table. It looked like a halo. I felt myself smiling stupidly.

Was he tilting to the left?

"Her drink," Cheryl said. Was it just me or was she slurring her words? "Something's wrong with it."

"I'd be happy to have the bartender make you another one." The waiter turned eager puppy eyes to me. No doubt worried about his tip.

"Why do you have two faces?" I blurted. They both stared at me like I was the one with two heads. "What? You have two faces, too." I pointed at Cheryl, my finger weaving in and out. "Oh, no. I've got two fingers." I held my finger up in front of me. Yep. Two. I turned to stare at the room. There was two of everything and they were spinning and spinning. I heard Cheryl shouting at the waiter to call an ambulance right about the time my face smacked into the table. That was gonna leave a mark.

# # #

I was heartily sick of waking up in hospitals. I was pretty sure they'd even put me in the same room as they had just a few months before. The nurse was definitely the same one. I recognized the glower as she loomed over me.

"Welcome back," she said sourly. "Getting to be a regular habit with you."

My mouth tasted like roadkill, and my throat felt like raw hamburger. "What happened?" I managed to croak.

"We had to pump your stomach. Looks like someone tried to kill you." She said the latter a little too cheerfully, as if the thought made her day.

"Bet you'd like that," I mumbled.

She snorted but otherwise didn't answer.

"How long have I been here?"

"Just since last night."

"What time is it?"

She muttered something under her breath about annoying patients who asked too many questions. Finally she said, "Just after eleven. In the morning."

"When can I blow this joint?" I tried to lift the blanket covering me, but I was weak as a half-drowned kitten.

"Can't be soon enough for me. The doc will be in here shortly. Hopefully he'll decide you can be discharged."

I frowned. "You're being awfully mean to a person who just nearly died."

She snorted again before stomping out the door without a backward glance. I grimaced. She could have at least handed me the TV remote. Or a toothbrush.

Cheryl came sailing in a moment later. She'd exchanged her red Chucks for blue ones and her gray hoodie for a pink one. Other than that, she looked the same as she had at the bar, complete with Wonder Woman t-shirt.

"Oh, good, you're awake. I brought muffins." She lifted a white paper bag and gave it a little shake. My stomach rolled.

"I'll pass, thanks."

Her eyes widened. "Doth my ears deceive me? Or are you passing on food?"

"Hey, I just had my stomach pumped. Be nice. Speaking of which, why did I have my stomach pumped?"

She perched on the edge of one of the visitor chairs and pulled a poppy seed muffin out of the bag. She nibbled on it while she told me the tale. "Seems somebody spiked your drink. Bat thinks it was a roofy, but it's possible it was poison of some kind. They've got to run tests."

"Who did it?"

"Bat's looking into that." Was it just me? Or was there a little sparkle in her eye when she mentioned his name? "One of the guys last night claimed he saw somebody put something in your drink. Why he didn't say anything at the time is beyond me." She gave a snort of disgust and popped another bite of muffin in her mouth. "But Bat's following up the leads, so we'll see."

"I won't hold my breath." It wasn't that I didn't trust Bat to find out who poisoned me. Fine. That was a lie. I totally didn't trust him. Bat had his own agenda and I had mine. And mine was to find out who was trying to kill me—and I had a pretty good idea who it was.

Shéa MacLeod

Chapter 20
Boyfriend Material

The doctor arrived nearly four hours later. By then, I was foaming at the mouth. Cheryl had refused to let me out of bed or to get me my clothes so I could get out of the hospital. Instead she'd sat mutinously by the bed and threatened to call back Nurse Ratched if I didn't behave.

After declaring me lucky to be alive, the doctor signed my release papers. I was just getting dressed when there was a knock at the door and Lucas poked his head in. "Anyone home?" There was a wary look in his eyes as if he wasn't sure of his welcome.

I paused in the act of buttoning my jeans. "What's he doing here?" I hissed at Cheryl.

"I told him what happened. Of course he came. He's in love with you, dummy."

I'd have to have a chat with Cheryl about poking her nose in my business. Later. For now I gave Lucas a half-hearted smile. "Just getting ready to bust out of here."

His lopsided grin was adorable. "I've got a getaway car if you need one."

That made me laugh. "Is it headed past a coffee shop? Because I could use some caffeine." Although I wasn't totally sure my stomach was up to it just yet, coffee was most definitely calling me loud and clear. Plus it would give us a chance to talk. Seemed like after the winery, we probably needed to get a few things straight.

Cheryl waved us goodbye and headed off to her laptop

and her work in progress while Lucas ushered me to his car. I felt grungy and overdressed. No doubt I looked like a raccoon since I hadn't had a chance to remove my makeup. My hair had definitely seen better days, and I was in dire need of a shower. Ah, well. If he couldn't handle me at my worst, he didn't deserve me anyway.

It had started to rain, and we drove in silence through the wet streets. Droplets occasionally splashed on the windshield, though it had turned to mist more than anything. Thick, gray billows of fog blocked the view of the river as fog horns rolled their mournful calls. The quiet felt awkward.

Finally Lucas pulled up to one of the many drive-thru coffee shops. He ordered a chai tea latte for himself and a toasted marshmallow latte for me. Plus two blueberry scones. Then without a word he drove to my house.

Lucas insisted on tucking me under an afghan on the couch before busying himself getting plates and whatnot for the scones. Finally he sat in the chair facing me, our drinks and food between us on the coffee table. I didn't say anything. I knew he was mad at me and probably expected an apology, but I wasn't sure there was one to be made. After all, I'd merely made use of the time. Two for one, so to speak. What was wrong with that? I couldn't let the opportunity escape me. I might not have had it again.

"We need to talk," he said finally.

I cringed. Those were four words that never boded well. Granted, I'd been reluctant about this whole relationship from the start. I liked my life. Liked being single. I'd created something that worked for me and adding a man to the mix... well, it hadn't gone well in the past. Men complicated things no matter how handsome and sexy they were. And no matter how great the chemistry or how many things you had in common.

He twisted his cup in his hands. Steam rose gently from the narrow opening in the lid. I held my breath, then expelled it with some force.

"Fine. Talk." It came out a little blunter than I meant. Getting aggressive wasn't the best move, but I was braced for a break-up and it just came out. I wished he'd get on with it and put me out of my misery.

Instead, he took my hand. "Viola, I'm worried about you."

That surprised me. "Why?"

"There's a killer out there and, thanks to your nosiness, he—or she—has decided you're a target."

Tell me something I don't know. "So? I'm not going to back down over a little danger."

"No, I don't suppose you will. But I want you to be careful."

"I'm always careful," I said stubbornly.

He gave me the eye.

"Fine. I'm mostly careful. I've done all right so far."

"So far," he agreed. "But things change and this could be the time that it all goes wrong."

"Or it could be the time that I catch the killer. Just like the last three times. Or have you forgotten?" He'd been there, after all. Granted, the last time had been an attempted killer rather than an actual killer, but the point remained.

"I haven't," he admitted. "I also haven't forgotten that you used our date as an excuse to badger a suspect."

"It was a coincidence. I had no idea she was going to be there. How could I? And how could I let the opportunity pass?"

"Easy," he said, sounding tired. "Ignore her. Let it go. Focus on us. She wasn't going anywhere. You could have gone back later."

I snorted. "You wouldn't say that to Bat."

"Bat is a police detective. It's his job. It's not yours."

He had me there. Still. "When you met me, I was in the middle of solving a murder. You even offered to help. What makes this different?"

"That was one time. Now it's becoming a habit, and you're constantly putting yourself in danger. Not to mention it's affecting our lives. We can't go out for an evening without you interrogating someone."

"So this is about you being jealous?"

His eyes widened and his cheeks colored angrily. "That's how you're going to twist this?"

"I'm not twisting anything," I snapped. "You're making this all about you. Have you forgotten my friend was murdered?" My voice steadily rose until I was almost yelling. I was so mad I could spit. "You think I'm just going to sit around and wait for the police to figure it out when my friends are dropping like flies? Is that what you would do?"

"No, but I'm..."

"What? A man?" Now I was furious. I yanked the

afghan back, jumped off the couch, stomped over, and yanked open the door. "I think you should leave."

"You've got it wrong," he said quietly. "This isn't about me being a man. It's about me being trained."

I blinked. "What are you talking about?"

"I was trained by the Israeli army."

Shéa MacLeod

Chapter 21
Revelations

"Say what?" I let go of the door.

"I'm part Jewish. When I was younger, I lived in Israel. I joined the Israeli army and served for several years in Special Forces."

I sat down. At some point I'd closed the door, though I didn't remember doing it. "Mossad?" I'd watched NCIS. I knew some things.

He nodded. "For a while. Believe me, I can take care of myself. You, on the other hand..." He reached out and took my hand in his. "You're vulnerable, and you're putting yourself in harm's way with no way to protect yourself. I can't always be there to help. Do you get where I'm coming from?"

I did. Of course I did. It was annoying, but I got it. I might be smart and maybe even sneaky, but I was in no way able to physically protect myself from someone bigger or stronger. "You could teach me," I blurted.

His eyebrows went up. "What?"

Now that I thought about it, it was a great idea. "Surely you know some self-defense moves. Or that krav whatever."

"Krav Maga?"

"Yeah. That's the one. You could teach me some moves."

He gave me a long look. "You're not going to stay out of trouble, are you?"

"Not a chance."

"Fine," he agreed. "I'll teach you some moves."

I grinned. "Excellent. When do we start?"

He took a sip of his chai. "When you're feeling better."

I pouted as I reached for my latte. "Spoil sport."

"And one other thing."

"Hmmm?"

"When we're on a date, there's no investigating. Not unless you tell me first and we agree on a plan. Promise?"

"Okay."

"Viola…" there was a warning edge to his tone.

"Hey, I'll do my best. That's all I can promise."

He groaned. "You are going to turn me gray, woman."

"Too late," I said cheerfully and kissed him.

# # #

Cheryl arrived at the house later that day practically buzzing with excitement. I was curled up on the couch with a cup of tea watching some awful afternoon TV. Lucas had returned to Portland for some meeting or other. He'd wanted to stay, but the meeting was important so I'd shooed him away with a promise to talk that night.

"Look." She handed me her cell phone. "I've got evidence."

"Of what?" I frowned at the screen. There was a picture of the inside of The Prohibition from what appeared to be the night before.

"So… remember I told you there was that guy who saw somebody put something in your drink?" she asked.

"Vaguely," I admitted as she plopped down on the couch next to me.

"Well, I remembered Kenny was celebrating his birthday last night and I just knew he would have taken tons of pictures."

"Okay." I had no idea who Kenny was.

"I had him send me the photos. Then I tracked down that guy."

"The one who saw someone spike my drink?"

She nodded.

"How did you manage that?" I asked.

She colored slightly. "I got his info from Bat."

"And what did you have to do to get the info?"

She turned redder. "I promised to have drinks with him."

I grinned. She glared.

"I thought after Duke you'd sworn off men."

"It's not men. It's just Bat," she said huffily. "Anyway. The witness works over at the Riverside Hotel, and I got him to look at the pictures. You'll never guess who he saw spike your drink."

"Madison," I said before she could even point out the culprit.

Her eyes widened. "How'd you know?"

"Call it a gut feeling."

Shéa MacLeod

Chapter 22
The Problem With Murder

"Hello, Madison." I slid into the booth next to her, effectively blocking her in. The diner was quiet as it was late for breakfast and still early for lunch.

"What the hell?" Madison snarled, sloshing a bit of coffee on the cheap, Formica table.

I tsked. "Language."

"What do you care about my language?"

I shrugged. "I'm a writer. I'm all about words. I'm also all about the truth."

She stared at me with a mulish expression. "What's that supposed to mean?"

"It means," I pulled out my phone and showed her the screen, "that last night you were at The Prohibition."

She stared at the photo. "So? Lots of people were at The Prohibition last night. It was Kenny's birthday."

How did she know Kenny and I didn't? Focus, Viola. "But lots of people did not have the opportunity to poison my drink. You did." I pointed to the image of a sullen Madison leaning on the counter next to a tray of drinks. Based on the martini glass and the copper mug, they were mine and Cheryl's.

"See," I said, tapping my finger on the screen. "How conveniently placed you are for dropping something right in that little mug."

"Just because I'm there doesn't mean I did it."

"Really? Then tell me, Madison. Who else would have

169

reason to poison me?"

She thrust out her lower jaw. "I don't know. Whoever killed my mother, maybe?"

I gave her a long, hard look.

"Oh, please," she sputtered. "I didn't kill anyone. Least of all my mother."

"Maybe not. But it seems awfully convenient that you were so close to my drink."

"I wasn't the only one," she snapped. "Plenty of people could have done it. I didn't. I just want you to stop."

I frowned. "Stop what? Trying to find the truth? You know how guilty that makes you look?"

Madison shrugged.

"Who are you covering for, Madison? Your boyfriend, maybe?"

She shot me a nasty glare. "I'm not covering for anyone. He didn't do it."

"Don't you want me to find out who killed your mom?"

"What does it matter?" There were tears in her eyes and for the first time I realized how deeply this all was affecting her. "It's too late. You can't bring her back."

"No. I can't. But I can bring her justice. I know you didn't kill her, and I want to prove it. I need to find out who did."

"You really don't think I did it?"

"Not anymore," I assured her. "Will you help me?"

She shrugged. "I don't see how I can."

"You're sure that your boyfriend wasn't involved?" I

asked.

"Absolutely not. I swear. He's the one that stopped me from going off on her."

Fair enough. I really hadn't thought he was guilty anyway. "Did you see anything? Anything at all unusual that day your mother died? Even the smallest thing."

"No. Nothing."

"No deliveries? No one knocked on the door?"

Madison's nose scrunched up a bit as she thought it over. "No. Nothing. I mean, mom was talking to Velma in the backyard kind of early. It woke me up and I was really pissed about it." She gave me a watery smile. "Seems stupid now."

"Velma Marx? The neighbor?"

"Yeah. They had some stupid rivalry going on about their rose bushes or something. I think they were yelling about cupcakes." She frowned. "I don't know. It was early and things are a little fuzzy."

"How interesting. I think it's time to visit Velma Marx."

# # #

Velma Marx lived in a cute little Victorian cottage right next door to Krys Marlowe's former residence. The siding was painted pale yellow, the trim purple, and the front porch sky blue to match the shutters. The ornate wrought iron fence surrounding the front yard was painted black except for the fleur-de-lis toppers, which were gold. The garden was prepped for the coming winter, but was always a stunning array of flowers in the summer. The whole thing was ridiculously picture perfect. I may have been a little jealous. I do not have a particularly green thumb. I mean, I manage, thanks to the occasional visit by a local landscaping company, but my yard had nothing on Velma's.

I rapped on the door and waited. The white lace curtains moved a little, and a round face appeared. Then it disappeared, and a moment later, the door swung open.

Velma gave me a cheerful smile that looked a little fake. Her white hair was a bit wild and unkempt and her horn-rimmed glasses were slightly askew. There were grass stains on her jeans.

"Been gardening?" I asked.

"Er..." she glanced down at her dirty jeans. "Oh, that. I was about to. How can I help you?"

"My name is Viola Roberts..."

"Oh, yes. You're one of those bunco girls."

I was surprised she knew me by that instead of by being a writer. "Um, yeah. How'd you know?"

"It was in the paper. I get the Astoria Gazette delivered, you know. Plus Agatha mentioned you once or twice."

"Uh, sure. Listen, I wanted to talk to you about Krys Marlowe."

"That woman?" Velma turned up her nose as if something smelled bad. "Why would you want to talk about that woman?"

"Because I'm trying to help the police find out who killed her."

"I'm sure the police don't need your help, dear."

Condescending much?

"Possibly not," I admitted. "But I do want to be a good citizen."

"Well, I don't know how I can help you."

"I was talking to Krys's daughter, Madison, and she said you visited Krys on the morning of her death. Very early."

"Well, we were neighbors. Can I help it if we run into each other now and then?"

"So it wouldn't have anything to do with the cupcake contest?" I asked.

Velma stiffened. I was on to something. "I don't know what you mean."

"I think you do. I think you were worried Krys was going to win the Cupcake Bake-off just like she's won the Garden Beautification Contest the last few years, so you decided to take her out."

"I didn't mean to kill her," Velma blurted. Then she slapped her hands over her mouth, horrified.

"So it was you!"

"I just meant to make her sick. She wouldn't be able to bake if she was sick. I figured I'd make her sick enough that she would miss the bake-off and someone else would have the chance to win."

"Someone like you, you mean."

Velma shrugged. "Maybe."

"Why did you spike my drink?" I demanded.

"Well, the bee didn't work."

I blinked. "What? You put the bee in my house?

Where did you get a bee in the middle of winter?"

Velma scowled. "It was meant for Ruby. She was deathly allergic to bees and I have a friend who's a bee keeper. I figured it would be perfect. Unfortunately, your name and hers are close to each other in Voss's records. I got them mixed up." She seemed very put out. "I put the bee in the wrong house."

"So you killed Ruby, too. Why?" Poor Ruby.

"She saw me putting the poison into Krys's stupid smoothie."

"How is that possible?" I asked, confused. Ruby had lived several blocks away. In fact, her house was a street over from my own. How could she have seen anything? "She was sick that day. That's why she couldn't come to bunco."

Velma scowled. "Well, maybe she was and maybe she wasn't, but she certainly took her morning constitutional. Stupid morning walking obsession. Every day she walked by my house at 8 AM on the dot. I figured I would have plenty of time to get into Krys's, doctor the drink, and get out. But for whatever reason, Ruby decided to walk early that day. She saw me go into the house and watched me through the window. She saw me poison Krys's smoothie. Anyway, I managed to convince her they were vitamins, but when Krys dropped dead that night, Ruby threatened to tell the police. I had to shut her up."

Which was when she'd put the bee in my place, mistaking it for Ruby's, thanks to the file mix-up. "So when the bee didn't work..."

"I doctored her salad." Velma actually seemed proud

of that.

Poor, poor Ruby. "And then you somehow slipped something into my drink."

"You were getting too close."

Actually, I'd been miles away, but I wasn't about to admit it. "I'm going to have to take you in," I told her.

"You're not the police," she scoffed, backing up.

"No, but they're on their way. I just sent Bat a text." I flashed my phone screen at her.

Velma let out a few words no lady should know and took off like a shot, shoving past me so hard I hit the porch with a jarring thud. I couldn't believe how quick she was for an old lady. She yanked open her car door, jumped in, and revved the engine. I scrambled to my feet and ran toward her car, but she backed up so fast, she nearly ran right over the top of me. Then she took off in a screech of tires.

Chapter 23
Car Chase

I stared after Velma's retreating car, the taillights flashing as she made a hard right turn. Well, hard-ish. She couldn't have been going more than twenty.

Shaking my head, I climbed into my own car. "Really, Velma? You're going to do this?" I revved the engine and took off after the octogenarian. I caught up with her easily. Her faded red Pinto didn't exactly blend in.

I tried to pull up alongside her, but she yanked her wheel to the left and tried to sideswipe me. Not willing to damage my paint job, I gave up and pulled in behind her, using my cell phone to call Bat.

"What is it now?" he asked in a long suffering tone.

"I'm in a low-speed car chase."

"Excuse me?"

"I know who killed Krys Marlowe and Ruby. It was Velma Marx."

There was a beat of silence. "You mean the old lady that lives next door to the Marlowes? The one who's obsessed with her garden?"

"Yep. She admitted the whole thing, then she jumped in her Pinto and took off. I'm following her."

"You're kidding."

"Unfortunately, no." I winced as Velma veered to miss a tourist and sideswiped a mailbox. One of those big blue ones. The Pinto was undamaged, but the box had a streak of tomato-soup-colored paint on it.

"She just damaged federal property. And—holy crap—she nearly wiped out the mayor!"

Charlie Bayles stared at us from the middle of the cross walk as we both zoomed by at a respectable twenty-five. Up ahead, the stop light was red. Was Velma going to stop?

"I can't believe this is my life," Bat muttered.

"Well, it's going to get messier if you don't get down here and stop her."

Velma coasted to a stop at the red light. I stopped close on her bumper. She held up her hand and flipped me off.

"Well, I never..."

"What?" Bat asked.

"She gave me the finger."

"What finger?"

"The middle finger, you idiot. What other finger?"

"That sweet old lady?" He actually seemed surprised.

"Need I remind you that sweet old lady just confessed to two murders?" I snapped. "Plus she tried to kill me. Twice. Well, the first time was an accident, but the second was definitely attempted murder."

"Lord, give me strength," he muttered. "Where are you?"

"We're on 14th Street." 14th was a one-way toward the Columbia River. "Just passed The Prohibition. Turning left on Marine right now. We're headed for the bridge."

"On my way." And he hung up.

With a shrug, I refocused on Velma as she pulled

cautiously onto Astoria's main drag. People stared as we drove slowly by, Velma in her red Pinto and me in my blue Toyota practically on her bumper. Every few blocks she'd slow down to a near standstill in order to flip me off again. I swear all we needed was the Benny Hill theme song playing in the background. It was that ridiculous.

We were nearly to the bridge when a squad car came screeching out of nowhere and pulled up to block Velma's path. She blasted her horn but the officer wouldn't budge. Velma coasted to a stop, rolled down the window, and shouted, "Move your car."

"Sorry, ma'am. Please turn off your engine and step out of the car," he said.

"I will not," Velma yelled out the window. "This is a getaway." She blasted her horn which sounded like a sick roadrunner.

The young officer stared at her, turned and gave me a look, then turned back to Velma. "Getaway is over ma'am. Get out of the car, please."

Velma wouldn't budge. Fortunately Bat arrived at that moment and managed to wrangle the elderly woman out of the Pinto and into the back of the squad car. Right behind Bat was a tow truck which promptly hooked up the Pinto and dragged it off. Velma flipped off the driver.

Bat stared at me. "I should site you for reckless driving."

"Just doing my duty as an upstanding citizen. Couldn't let a murderer get away, now could I?"

He gritted his teeth. "I don't know how you do it."

I shrugged. "It's a gift."

Chapter 24
Much Ado About Motives

"I can't believe that sweet old woman murdered two people," Cheryl said as she tossed the dice. They rattled across the table. Six, five, four. Too bad we weren't playing cards. That would have been the start of a good hand. "How exactly did she manage it?"

"Apparently she knew about Krys Marlowe's habit of mixing up a big weekly batch of green smoothies and drinking one every morning. She just snuck into the house and put some hemlock juice in with the smoothie mix."

"Good grief." Agatha shook her head, her red-beaded earrings making a little tinkling noise. "And poor Ruby. She saw Velma do it?"

"Yep," I said. "According to Velma, when Ruby saw Velma sneaking into Krys's house, she got curious. She snuck into the garden and peered through the window in time to see Velma putting the hemlock in the smoothie. Whether Ruby truly realized what she'd seen or not, we'll never know, but Velma was convinced she had to get rid of Ruby before she went to the cops. A little hemlock leaf in Ruby's salad, and it was all over."

"I still don't understand why she put a bee in your house," Cheryl said. "That's just… weird."

"She thought it was Ruby's house," I explained. "Velma broke into Dr. Voss's office because she wanted a way to kill Ruby without alerting the police. She thought she struck gold when she read about Ruby's bee allergy."

"But how did she get your houses mixed up?" Agatha asked.

"Apparently when she was rifling through the files," I continued, "she heard a siren, got scared, and stuffed the file back into the drawer. But the car went right on by, so she went back to the file to get Ruby's address—never having been to Ruby's house before. Ruby Rogers is right next to Viola Roberts in the files, and she pulled the wrong one. She got the address and didn't bother to look further. Then she put a bee in my house, thinking it was Ruby's. She expected Ruby to die of anaphylactic shock from the bee sting. The cops would chalk it up to an act of nature and move on, never connecting it to Krys's death."

"That's insane," Agatha said. "If not a little brilliant. She is over eighty, you know." As if being an octogenarian made murdering someone clever.

I took my turn with the dice. "Even crazier is why she did it. Because of that stupid cupcake contest. She thought Krys was going to win."

Agatha picked up my thrown dice and took her turn, the dice thudding lightly against the card table. "That Velma won the garden contest for the last nine years running before Krys Marlowe came to town. And she won the pie eating contest every year, too."

"You had a pie eating contest?" I asked. "And Velma won?"

"You wouldn't believe how much food that old woman can put away," Agatha said. "You'd have thought she could have let someone else win something for once." She sighed. "The woman always did have a screw loose. Poor Ruby."

"Yeah, poor Ruby," I agreed.

"At least the bunco ladies have been exonerated," Agatha pointed out. "That's something."

I wasn't sure Bat had ever seriously considered them suspects, but I let it go. They all seemed overly thrilled with the thought they'd been Persons of Interest.

"And I'm glad I could help out," Agatha said with a proud smile. "You should have me along on your investigations more often."

Cheryl and I exchanged horrified glances.

Agatha solving crime. Yeah, that was all we needed.

The End

Read on for a sample of the next book in the Viola Roberts Cozy Mystery series, *The Venom in the Valentine*:

Chapter 1

"Now that's what I call stunning." My best friend, Cheryl Delaney, dropped her bags in the middle of the hotel room and stared out the large picture window.

Beyond the glass pane, the ocean heaved itself up onto the dark rocks edging the beach, sending white plumes high into the air. Dark clouds scudded along in the sky above, while pines tossed wildly in the wind below. February along the Oregon Coast tended toward the wild side.

"I still can't believe Lucas ditched you, Viola." Cheryl didn't turn around, her gaze still on the surging surf below. "And on Valentine's, too. Such a shame. Still, his loss is my gain!"

I scowled. "Lucas didn't ditch me. His flight was delayed. He'll be here on the day."

Like me, my boyfriend, Lucas Salvatore, was a writer. In fact, we'd met at a writer's conference in Florida and the rest, as they say, was history. Unlike me, he was the sort of writer whose novels got made into movies, so he was in demand as a speaker at conferences all over the world. Unfortunately, a snowstorm on the East Coast had grounded flights and left him stranded three thousand miles from home just a few short days before the Big V: Valentine's Day. It was supposed to be our first as a couple. We'd planned to spend it at The Grand Seaview Resort, one of Oregon's most romantic ocean side hotels. Instead of canceling, Lucas insisted Cheryl take his place. Hopefully he'd be able to join later. I wasn't holding my breath.

"This actually works out great for me," I said, setting my own suitcase carefully on the rack provided.

"Really? How's that?"

"Well." I unzipped my case and began carefully unpacking. I was a nester, and hated living out of a suitcase. I didn't feel at home until my shirts were in the top drawer and my pants in the bottom. You know how it is. "I've got proofs due on my latest novel, *The Rancher's Ransomed Bride*. This way I don't have to feel guilty about working on it over Valentine's."

This time Cheryl did turn. "Viola Roberts!" She propped her hands on her hips and glared at me. "We're here to relax, not work."

I hid a smirk. An angry Cheryl was a bit like an enraged pixie: adorable and hard to take seriously. Her short, spiky dark hair only added to the image. She was a smidge shorter than my own five foot five and delicately slender where I was voluptuous and curvy. Cheryl was also a writer, though her forte was mysteries and thrillers where mine was historical romances of the Old West variety. Which meant lots of ranchers and cowboys and mail order brides.

Cheryl and I had met shortly after I moved to Astoria, Oregon and joined the local writers' group. We'd hit it off immediately. And, although we'd both left the original group, we'd remained fast friends.

"I know we're here to relax, and I will, but I've got to finish the proofs first. They're due on V-Day."

She scowled, a line forming between her brows. "You should tell your editor to hold her britches. This is a holiday."

"I'll get right on that." Since my publisher was me, I had no intention of listening. Deadlines were deadlines. Otherwise I'd never get anything done. Besides, I was so used to spending Valentine's Day alone, the idea that I actually had someone to celebrate with this year was…unnerving.

"Fine," she said sulkily. "Let's go get a drink at the bar, at least. Then you can get to your precious proofs."

"Thank you." Part of me itched to get started, but another part of me could really use that drink. Driving down the coast from Astoria had been a little harrowing, thanks to the wind. More than once I'd imagined us plummeting—car and all—over the edge of Highway 101 and into the sea. I have way too much imagination for my own good.

Our suite was one of the very best, on the top floor, so we took the elevator to the lobby. The large area was dotted with clusters of sofas and comfy chairs. The open space was meant for guests to sit and relax while enjoying the view from the floor to ceiling windows spanning the entire front of the building. Few were interested at the view as the panes were splatted with drops of moisture, and the sky loomed dark and ominous.

"Looks like a storm," Cheryl said. "Let's sit near the fire."

"Sure."

Off in one corner was a massive fireplace of local river stone. A real wood fire radiated tremendous amounts of heat. Cheryl didn't seem to mind, but I, on the other hand, immediately broke out in a sweat. I moved my chair a little ways back to avoid the worst of the heat.

In another corner was a small bar serving bottles of beer and glasses of wine. No hard liquor or mixed cocktails. Which was a shame as I fancied my favorite: blackberry bourbon. Instead I ordered a rich Malbec while Cheryl chose a lighter Pinot. I had to admit, relaxing with a glass of wine in front of a roaring fire while a storm raged outside was just what the doctor ordered. I was half tempted to forget those proofs.

"Are these seats taken?"

I glanced up to find a middle aged man and someone I assumed was his wife. He was dressed in neatly pressed khaki's and a blue button-down shirt. He looked like the briefcase carrying kind. Lawyer, maybe.

"Not at all. Have a seat." I waved magnanimously.

"I'm Lawrence Tupper—you can call me Larry—and this is my wife, Angie. We're here to celebrate our twenty-sixth wedding anniversary." He gave me a wide smile. He was an attractive man, for his age, with pure, white hair and sparkling blue eyes. He had only a small paunch around the middle.

"Congratulations!" Cheryl beamed happily and raised her glass in a toast.

"Thank you," Angie said. Her hair was dark and sleek—bottle, no doubt—and her age carefully hidden beneath a thick layer of makeup. From the tautness around her eyes and throat, I was guessing there'd been a face lift or two involved. Her smile seemed fake, never reaching her eyes, and I wondered if she really wanted to be here. "How long have you been together?" she asked.

I stared at her, confused for a moment. "Oh, we're not a couple. We're best friends. For over three years now."

"I apologize. I just assumed... You know, with it being Valentine's Day and all." Angie looked away, clearly embarrassed.

"Don't worry about it," I said with a wave of my hand. The wine was sending a warm glow through me and I was feeling relaxed and happy. "We know each other so well, it's an easy mistake." It was kind of funny though, since Cheryl could be downright boy crazy. When she wasn't on one of her dating moratoriums. She didn't have the best luck when it came to men.

"It's nice that you can celebrate your wedding anniversary here," Cheryl said. "It seems like such a romantic hotel."

"Very," Larry said. "That's why I chose it. Though it is a bit out of the way."

He wasn't kidding about that. The fifty year-old luxury resort had been built about half-way between two towns—Lincoln City and Newport—smack dab on the ocean in the middle of nowhere. You had to drive down a narrow, winding drive to get to it. It had its own restaurant, spa, and work-out room as well as a small golf course. There was no reason to leave the resort unless you wanted to, and during the stormy season—which was now—it could become quite isolated.

"It's perfect for a romantic getaway," Cheryl assured him.

"Did anyone ever tell you that you look just like Halle Berry?" Larry asked.

"No, never," Cheryl lied politely. She only got that line from just about everyone she met. "How sweet of you."

"She looks nothing like Halle Berry," Angie said tartly.

There was a flash of something in her eyes. Jealousy, perhaps? Her reaction was odd, because Larry hadn't been flirting with Cheryl. He'd just been complimentary. The entire time he'd held his wife's hand as if he couldn't bear to let her go. Was she just insecure? Or was there something deeper going on?

Perhaps you're right," Larry said soothingly. "Oh, look. Our reservations are in an hour. We should get ready. Ladies, if you'll excuse us?"

We murmured our goodbyes. Angie didn't even look our way. Definitely something odd with that woman.

I reminded myself firmly that I was there to relax and finish my proofs. Not get all up in someone else's business. Still, Angie Tupper's reaction remained with me the rest of the evening.

The Venom in the Valentine is available Now.

The Venom in the Valentine – Chapter One
Text copyright © 2017 Shéa MacLeod
All rights reserved.
Printed in the United States of America.

The Body in the Bathtub

Note from Shéa

Thank you for reading. If you enjoyed this book, I'd appreciate it if you'd help others find it so they can enjoy it too.

- Lend it: This e-book is lending-enabled, so feel free to share it with your friends, readers' groups, and discussion boards.

- Review it: Let other potential readers know what you liked or didn't like about the story.

Book updates can be found at www.sheamacleod.com

The Body in the Bathtub

About Shéa MacLeod

Shéa MacLeod is the author of the bestselling paranormal series, Sunwalker Saga, as well as the award nominated cozy mystery series Viola Roberts Cozy Mysteries. She has dreamed of writing novels since before she could hold a crayon. She totally blames her mother.

She resides in the leafy green hills outside Portland, Oregon where she indulges in her fondness for strong coffee, Ancient Aliens reruns, lemon curd, and dragons. She can usually be found at her desk dreaming of ways to kill people (or vampires). Fictionally speaking, of course.

The Body in the Bathtub

Other Books by Shea Shéa MacLeod

Viola Roberts Cozy
Mysteries
The Corpse in the Cabana
The Stiff in the Study
The Poison in the Pudding
The Body in the Bathtub
The Remains in the
Rectory

Notting Hill Diaries
To Kiss a Prince
Kissing Frogs
Kiss Me, Chloe
Kiss Me, Stupid
Kissing Mr. Darcy

Cupcake Goddess
Novelettes
Be Careful What You Wish
For
Nothing Tastes As Good
Soulfully Sweet
A Stich in Time

Dragon Wars
Dragon Warrior
Dragon Lord
Dragon Goddess
Green Witch

Sunwalker Saga
Kissed by Blood
Kissed by Darkness
Kissed by Fire
Kissed by Smoke
Kissed by Moonlight
Kissed by Ice
Kissed by Eternity
Kissed by Destiny

Sunwalker Saga: Soulshifter
Trilogy
Fearless
Haunted
Soulshifter

Sunwalker Saga: Witch
Blood Series
Spellwalker
Deathwalker
Mistwalker (coming Fall
2016)

Omicron ZX
Omicron Zed-X: Omicron
ZX prequel Novellette
A Rage of Angels

13286194R00124

Made in the USA
San Bernardino, CA
13 December 2018